4 books in 1!

4 books in 1!

Too Much Space!

Party Crashers

Take Us to Your Sugar

Double Trouble

written and illustrated by Jonathan Roth

ALADDIN

New York   London   Toronto   Sydney   New Delhi

ALADDIN

An imprint of Simon & Schuster Children's Publishing Division
1230 Avenue of the Americas, New York, New York 10020
This Aladdin edition September 2019
Too Much Space! copyright © 2018 by Jonathan Roth
Party Crashers copyright © 2018 by Jonathan Roth
Take Us to Your Sugar copyright © 2018 by Jonathan Roth
Double Trouble copyright © 2018 by Jonathan Roth
Cover illustrations copyright © 2018 by Jonathan Roth

For information about special discounts for bulk purchases, please contact
Simon & Schuster Special Sales at 1-866-506-1949 or business@simonandschuster.com.
The Simon & Schuster Speakers Bureau can bring authors to your live event. For more
information or to book an event contact the Simon & Schuster Speakers Bureau
at 1-866-248-3049 or visit our website at www.simonspeakers.com.
Series designed by Nina Simoneaux
The illustrations for this book were rendered digitally.
The text of this book was set in Adobe Caslon Pro.
Manufactured in the United States of America 0719 FFG
2 4 6 8 10 9 7 5 3 1
Library of Congress Control Number 2019931781
ISBN 978-1-5344-5394-4
ISBN 978-1-4814-8854-9 (*Too Much Space!* eBook)
ISBN 978-1-4818-8857-0 (*Party Crashers* eBook)
ISBN 978-1-4814-8860-0 (*Take Us to Your Sugar* eBook)
ISBN 978-1-4814-8863-1 (*Double Trouble* eBook)
These titles were previously published individually.

★ CONTENTS ★

Too Much Space!

SPLOG ENTRY #1
A Horrible Place Called Space

Dear Kids of the Past,

Hi. My name's Bob and I live and go to school in space. That's right, space. Pretty sporky, huh? I'm the new kid this year at Astro Elementary, the only school in orbit around one of the outer planets. There's just one micro little problem:

SPACE IS THE MOST TERRIFYING PLACE EVER!

If you've been to space, you know what I mean: It's dark, cold, airless—and it goes on for infinity! Okay, maybe it ends at some super huge wall. But what's behind that wall? More space? Bigger walls? Giant space *spiders*?!

Just kidding about that last one. There are no spiders in space.

Are there?

No really, are there?

Beep just said to say hi. Beep is a young alien who got separated from his 600 siblings when they

 were playing hide-and-seek in some asteroid field. Then he floated around the void for a while, until he ended up here. Sad, huh?

★ 4 ★

You know what's even sadder? I was the one who found him knocking on our space station's air lock door and let him in. Now he thinks I'm his new mother!

On the bright side, everyone at school says Beep is super cute and fun to have around. And since he won't leave my side, they let him join my class as the school's first alien student. He's definitely a quick learner—he picks up languages in no time, and his grades are already better than mine!

Anyway, I'm writing these space logs (or splogs, as we call them) partly to tell you all about my hectic life, but mostly because it's an assignment to show you how "great" things are here in the future. At the end of each week I'll put all my entries into a time-velope and mail it to 200 years ago. If you receive this, please write back; and while you're at it, please also include a pile of vintage twenty-first-century comic books! Thanks.

Beep will help with the pictures. He's super talented and loves to draw, though in his excitement he sometimes eats all his pencils.

Hope you enjoy!

SPLOG ENTRY #2
Space Spiders!

Astro Elementary is a big space station orbiting Saturn. I think they picked Saturn because it looks cool in the brochures.

Trust me, I tried to get out of coming here. When I took the big admissions test, I filled out *C* for every answer. Instant fail, right?

Wrong! Turns out I was the only

kid on the planet this time to get a perfect score. Now everyone thinks I'm some kind of super space genius. I'm a failure even at failing! My parents were more surprised than anything, but as much as I begged, they wouldn't let me stay home *or* send my little sister in my place. She seemed particularly happy to see me go.

Beep and I share a dorm room in the living section of the station. Class starts promptly at 8:00 a.m., so we sleep in until about 7:55, then quickly float through the curved halls to our classroom. (Since there's no gravity in space, we have to float *every*where.)

Professor Zoome is our teacher. She begins each day by taking attendance.

"Zenith?" she called this morning.

"Here," Zenith said.

"Flash?"

"Here."

"Blaster?"

"Here."

(Everyone in my class has pretty cool space names.)

"Bob?"

"Here," I said. (Okay, so not *everyone*.)

When she was done, Professor Zoome clasped her hands together and said, "Class, I have some very good news. After you finish your morning splog entries, we're going on a field trip!"

This time last year, when I was still in school on Earth, we had a field trip where we went on a hayride. I love hayrides!

"To Pluto!" she added.

"Pluto?" I gulped. Pluto didn't have hayrides. It probably didn't even have ponies.

"No class has ever been on a field trip to Pluto before," Professor Zoome continued, "so it is very important to select a responsible partner. It should be someone you can share notes with, as well as someone who will risk life and limb to save you in any one of a billion probable space emergencies."

Double gulp.

Beep bounced up and down. "Pick Beep, Bob-mother!" he said. "Pick Beep!"

As if I had a choice.

"Okay, time to go," Professor Zoome said when we were done with our splogs a few minutes later. "Everyone to the Astrobus. Blastoff in five minutes!"

I don't know what Astrobuses were like in your time, but these days they're the pits. They smell like a mix of nuclear waste and peanut butter (and I'm allergic to peanuts).

"Beep call window!" Beep said as we floated aboard. I still wasn't used to all this floating, and it was definitely making me dizzy.

Once we had taken a seat, Beep pressed his face against the glass. "Saturn rings pretty," he said. "Go round and round and round and . . ."

Make that *very* dizzy.

I looked away, just in time to see my classmate Lani floating down the bus aisle. Lani is short for Laniakea Supercluster (which is a cluster of more than 100,000 galaxies, including ours). Not that I looked her up or anything. And even if I did, it was only because I wanted to learn more about her cool space name. Because I'm, you know, totally into everything about, uh, space.

Lani grabbed a handrail, coming to a stop.

"Hey, Zenith," she said to her partner, "let's sit by Beep and Bob!"

Zenith shrugged. "It's the only seat left anyway."

They settled in directly across the aisle. "Hey, Bob," Lani said. "How's it going?"

"Um. Um. Um . . ."

Before I could finish my thought, Beep popped up. "Why Bob-mother face so red? Too much hot in bus? Too much radioactive? Too much—"

I put my hand over his mouth.

Beep removed my hand and buckled his belt. "There yet?"

"We haven't left," I replied.

"Yet?" he said a second later.

"Pluto is billions of miles away, Beep. It'll take at least twenty minutes."

"Beep want snack."

Snacks happen to be a true passion of mine. Unfortunately, my stomach lurches about twelve different warp zones every time an Astrobus takes off. "In a minute," I said, trying not to hurl. Hurling in zero gravity is super unsporky.

The moment we leveled off, I scrolled through the Servo-server options on the seat back, but all they had left were orange-swirl ice pops and salt-free peanuts. I ordered an ice pop and it instantly shot up through a tube.

"Beep too!" Beep said. In seconds, his tongue was orange and the ice pop had disappeared. "Again!"

"We're only allowed to get one," I said. "Next time eat slower."

"Beep want next ice pop bigger!" he said.

"That's the only size they have."

He pouted for a moment, then leaned over me to stare at Lani, who was removing a jar from her backpack. The jar was buzzing.

"Snack?" Beep asked.

"Not for you, Beep," she said. "These are houseflies. For my latest science experiment."

"Huh?" Beep said.

Now that I was feeling better, I decided to play it cool and show Lani that maybe I was a smart astro guy after all. "Lani is obviously studying the controlled effects of zero gravity on tiny Earth insects that are used to flying in the confines of an atmosphere."

Pretty impressive, huh?

"Actually," Lani said, "the flies are only here to feed the subjects in my other jar: spiders."

(Note: those lines = me fainting.)

When I opened my eyes, Lani's face was spinning. Kind of like Saturn's rings. "What . . . what happened?" I said.

"You fainted when you saw my spiders," she said, holding them up again.

Okay, so maybe I had a slight fear of spiders. But she didn't have to keep shoving them in my face.

"Beep like spiders," Beep said.

Lani leaned forward. "Me too. They're actually my pets: Alpha, Beta, and Zilly. They're cute, friendly—unless you're a fly—and extremely smart. Look at their webs."

I peeked. The first two spiders had written complicated math equations. The third seemed more like an animal lover.

"They used to live in the ceiling of a lab where

there were lots of gamma blasts," Lani explained. "And I think the energy made them geniuses. That's how they can write messages like that. Though I don't always understand Zilly."

"Some pig!" Beep repeated.

"Some creepy insects," I corrected.

"Actually, spiders are arthropods," Lani went on, "of the order Araneae. There are tons of interesting things about them, such as—"

Luckily, Professor Zoome's voice boomed over the overhead speaker: "Prepare for landing," she said. "Dwarf planet approaching fast!"

SPLOG ENTRY #3
Ice Not Nice

Correction: *We* were the ones approaching fast. Though I guess Pluto was going fast too, in a relative way. In space everything goes fast. The Astrobus landed with the normal amount of smoothness, which is equal to riding a triple corkscrew roller coaster inside of a giant blender on top of a free-falling elevator.

"Now, kids," Professor Zoome said, "Pluto may be

small and cute, but it's far from cuddly. Nearly all its surfaces are icy, and its atmosphere is a thin layer of silent but deadly gasses."

We all chuckled at that one.

"Furthermore, it is dark, cold, and you have an eighty-eight percent chance of getting hopelessly lost if you don't follow directions. Unfortunately, our Astrobus's air lock can only hold one student at a time. So who wants to leave the bus first?"

Wait, did she say 88 percent chance of getting lost? That only left a 22 percent chance of *not* getting lost! Or was it 11 percent? Or . . .

I started counting on my fingers. But, to my shock, instead of counting, my hand shot up.

"Thank you, Bob," Professor Zoome said. "That's very brave of you to volunteer."

"But . . . but . . . !" I said, trying to pull my hand down. That's when I realized it was being held up by Blaster, who was in the seat behind me. I finally yanked it free.

"Good luck, space wimp!" Blaster chuckled. His buddy Atom chuckled too.

Blaster, I should mention, kind of doesn't like me. I should also mention he's about the size of a small moon.

I sighed and stood up. I then grabbed a space suit and helmet from the rack in back and slowly made my way up front.

"Don't forget your Visor Light," Professor Zoome said when I was suited up.

"Check," I said.

"Or your Emergency Space Pack."

"Check."

"Or your Secret Astronaut Diaper Kit."

"Uh, check."

I opened the hatch and took a deep breath. "This is one small step for a kid," I said, "one giant leap for gaaaaaaaaaaaaaaaaaaaaaaaaaaaaaaaaaaaaaaaaaaaaah!"

"Most importantly, don't forget to switch out your Space Boots for Ice Boots!" she called.

Now she tells me!

I had stepped onto slick whitish-orange ice and was now sliding downhill at about a hundred miles per hour. Toward what? Who knows? Probably more ice!

I pretty much thought I was dead, until— miracle of miracles—my field trip partner popped up beside me, foot surfing the ice like a pro. "Beep go wheeeeeeeeeeeeeeeeeeeeeeeeee!" he said.

The cool thing about Beep is that he adapts instantly to any environment, so he never has to wear space suits or anything (and I do mean *any*thing—you think all that bluish rubbery stuff on his body is *clothes*?).

"*Help!*" I cried. But somehow he thought that meant "help me go faster," so he gave me a push.

Pluto has a small amount of gravity, but it wasn't nearly enough to slow me down. I sped farther and farther along, sliding up and down icy hills until I finally came to a stop at the bottom of a deep crater.

Beep did a perfect triple flip and landed on his feet. "Pluto fun! Beep go again?"

"I have a better idea," I said. "Get me out of here!"

Beep handed me my Ice Boots, which I put on. Once I

climbed to the top of the crater, I stopped to catch my breath. The bus was a yellow dot on the horizon.

Beep's eyes were wide. "Zowwie," he said. "Bob see what Beep see?"

I stared at the vast white and orange landscape. "Yeah—ice."

"Not ice." He began to bounce. "Ice *pop!*"

Leave it to Beep to turn the dwarfiest planet into the largest treat. He dove back into the crater and began licking its sides.

"Yum!" he slurped. "Taste like orange-swirl!"

"Are you serious?" I asked.

"Bob-mother try!"

"I think I'll pass."

"Enough for *both* Beep and Bob-mother."

"Enough for the whole galaxy," I said. "But I'll still pass."

He shrugged. "Suit self."

I waited for him to stop, but he showed no signs of slowing. And that's when it hit me: If Beep was right, and Pluto was edible, he had just made a major scientific discovery. And you know what a major new scientific discovery means?

"Money!" I cried. "Beep, you're incredible. We'll open the biggest ice pop stand in the solar system. We're going to be *rich*!"

Pluto suddenly wasn't looking so bad. In fact, it was starting to look quite tasty.

"Guess I'll try a little after all," I said with a smile. "You know, just to make sure."

Even with my space suit's special trademark GasAway! fan filter, I knew I could only open my visor for a few minutes before the fumes would knock me out and the cold would make an ice pop out of *me*. But I didn't need much time. Just enough for one little lick.

I slid back down into the crater to join him. "Okay, Beep. Here goes."

I popped open my visor.

And stuck out my tongue.

And licked the ice.

That's when I made two of the most horrific scientific discoveries in history:

One: Pluto does *not* taste like orange-swirl. Not even close. Beep had only thought it did because the ice was orange and—as I'd sadly forgotten—his taste-receptors are *in his eyes*. And,

Two: MY TONGUE WAS TOTALLY STUCK!!!!!!!!!!!!!!!!!!!!!!!!!!!!!

SPLOG ENTRY #4:
Hurts the Force Does

So there I was: tongue stuck to the ice. A deadly chill seeping into my bones. And a really terrible itch forming in that one little spot on my back I could never, ever reach!

Luckily, I had a field trip partner, sworn to save me in one of a billion probable space emergencies.

Well, this is Beep in an epic space emergency: BOUNCE, BOUNCE, BOUNCE, *SHRIEK*.

BOUNCE, BOUNCE, BOUNCE, *SHRIEK.*

BOUNCE, BOUNCE, BOUNCE, *SHRIEK.*

Not super helpful.

I called his name: "'Eepth!"

I called for help: "'Elpth!"

He kept bouncing. I was doomed! And I was going to be known galaxy-wide as "The Kid Who Licked Pluto."

If only I had an Emergency Space Pack.

And that's when it hit me: I did!

I slipped it off and fumbled for the pocket labeled UNIVERSAL INTERSTELLAR DISTRESS SIGNAL BEACON DEVICE. Thank the stars! I pulled it out.

It was a whistle.

Okay, not to worry. Surely there had to be *some-*thing in the Emergency Space Pack I could use. I

dumped all the contents
onto the ice. And saw:

—an old Galaxy Scout
Compass

—three smiley face
Band-Aids

—a bottle of that fizzy,
stingy wound-
cleaning stuff

—a Temporary Shrink Ray

—a Temporary Giganticizer Ray

—a mini pack of Kleenex

—a mini hot water bottle

—a number 2 pencil

—a sewing kit

—an extra space suit button, and

—a Self-Destruct Button

Wait. Self-Destruct Button? Who put *that* there?!

I turned to Beep one last time. It was up to him now. Maybe, just maybe, if he put his little alien mind to it, he could combine all those useless emergency items to build some kind of super communication device that could . . .

BOUNCE, BOUNCE, BOUNCE, *SHRIEK.*

BOUNCE, BOUNCE, BOUNCE, *SHRIEK.*

BOUNCE, BOUNCE, BOUNCE, *SHRIEK.*

Okay, so I really *was* doomed.

"Bob-mother! Bob-mother!" he said. "They come! They come!"

And that's when I understood: Beep had been calling for help the whole time!

"We're coming, we're coming!" a voice called.

"Hey, it's Bob," Atom said, poking his head into the crater.

I was saved!

"And he's . . . oh, man, Blaster, get over here. Wait till you see this!"

Or not.

Out of the corner of my eye, I could see a crowd gathering at the crater's rim.

"'Elpth?" I squeaked.

"Everyone, move back, move back!" Blaster said. "We only have moments to act!" So maybe Blaster had a good side after all.

Then a camera flashed. "Got it!" Blaster said. "Priceless! This is so going on my splog."

Or not.

I began to feel woozy. Just then Beep bounced into view, yelling, "Free Bob-mother! Free Bob-mother!"

"You're his partner," Blaster said. "Why don't *you* free him?"

Beep only repeated, "Free Bob-mother! Free Bob-mother!"

Blaster sighed. "Fine, you little space-troll. But he's stuck pretty bad. There's only one thing we can do now. And that's to"—he paused dramatically—"use the Force."

Of course, the Force! With the Force you could do anything. As long as you were some kind of thousand-year-old master, that is.

Suddenly, two giant arms wrapped around me. Blaster's. And before I could stop him, he began to pull me free. With all *the force* he could muster.

"Gaaaaaaaaaaaaaaaaaaaaaaaaaaaaaaaaaaaaaaaaaaaaa aaaaaaaaaaah!" I screamed, nearly fainting from the pain in my tongue.

"Stop!" someone called. "What are you doing?" It sounded like Lani.

"Just trying to help," Blaster said.

"Yeah, right," Lani said, rushing down and pushing him off. "If you really wanted to help, you'd be using your Emergency Space Pack."

Blaster made a face. "The stuff in those is useless," he said. I kind of had to agree.

"Boys," Lani muttered. She grabbed the mini hot water bottle, punctured it with the pencil, and poured the hot water onto my tongue. Instantly, I stumbled back, free.

Why hadn't *I* thought of that?

Beep jumped over and hugged me. "Lani-friend save Bob-mother! Bob-mother owe life!"

Lani folded her arms. "What were you doing anyway? You could have been iced."

I tried to explain, but my numb, sore tongue made it difficult: "Luh luh uh luh uh luh."

"I don't understand."

I pointed to Beep. "Luh luh uh luh!"

Beep immediately began slurping the ground. "Yum yum orange-swirl!" he said.

Lani smiled. "Aw, isn't Beep cute."

And that was my field trip to Pluto.

SPLOG ENTRY #5:
LUH!

The rest of the trip was fairly uneventful. When we got back to school that afternoon, Professor Zoome called the school nurse, then told me to float straight to the health office.

"Luh!" I said. That translates to: "But I don't *want* to go to the health office. Nurse Lance is scary, and he always tries to give you a *shot*, even when you just have a laser-skinned knee, and anyway, my tongue doesn't hurt *that* bad anymore, I'm sure I'll be able to talk again in about eight or ten light-years." (Though, are light-years time or *distance*? I always forget.)

Professor Zoome pointed. "Feel better."

Beep, of course, tagged along. "Beep sorry Bob-mother dying. Beep have Bob-mother comics when Bob-mother gone?"

"Luh luh!" Beep wasn't *touching* my vintage twenty-first-century comics!

Nurse Lance was waiting for me. "Have a seat," he said, and I floated into the cold metal chair. He strapped me in. "Okay, so are you the student who needs ten space-sickness booster shots or the one who requires a painless, soothing, healing spray to the tongue?"

I opened my mouth wide and pointed with both hands, so he'd be sure to get it. "Luh!"

"Got it," he said. He began preparing a foot-long needle.

"So would you prefer all ten shots on one cheek? Or five on each?"

"LUHHHHHHH!" I screamed. Which cheeks was he talking about anyway?

He pointed the needle at my bottom. "Good

choice. Now, hold still. This will definitely sting. But if you don't pass out, you can have a lollipop. I have raspberry or orange-swirl. Do you have a favorite?"

Beep clapped. "Orange-swirl! Orange-swirl!"

Nurse Lance saw Beep's orange tongue. "Ah, so you must be the one who injured his tongue on Pluto."

"Beep no hurt tongue," Beep said. "Only get brain freeze from lick ice."

Luckily, I remembered my splog writing pad was clipped to my side. I quickly snapped it off and wrote: *NO SHOTS! I AM THE ONE WITH THE HURT TONGUE! ME!* ME!

Nurse Lance squinted. "Oh. So you are. Whyever didn't you say?" He put down the needle—whew!—and showed me two small spray bottles. "Would you like your painless, soothing, healing spray in lemon or lime flavor?"

Beep bounced. "Orange-swirl! Orange-swirl!"

Nurse Lance scowled. "It only comes in lemon or lime."

I pointed. "Luh."

"Lemon. Excellent choice. Open."

I did. *Squirt.* In a second it was over. And he was right. It was painless and soothing, if disgusting.

"I can talk!" I said.

Nurse Lance released me from the chair. "Works every time." He turned to Beep. "As for you: Let's see what we can do about that brain freeze."

Beep clapped. "More ice pop!"

Nurse Lance shook his head. "Not until you get your treatment." He rummaged around and pulled out a spray bottle that said FREEZE B GONE (TO WARM YOUR CHILLY BRAIN). "Ah, knew I had it somewhere. Specially formulated for aliens *only*. One squirt of this on your head, and you can eat all the ice pops you want."

Nurse Lance handed Beep the bottle, and Beep turned and squirted it. On *me*!

"Ow, Beep! That stings! You got it in my eyes!"

Nurse Lance grabbed the bottle back. "What are you doing? I said this formula is meant for *aliens*."

Beep pointed at me. "Alien."

"I'm not the alien, Beep. You are!"

"*BEEP* alien?"

"It tingles," I said as I tried to wipe the rest of the spray off my head.

"Oh, it's probably just seeping into your brain," Nurse Lance said. "On the bright side, the side effects should be only temporary."

"Wait, side effects? What side effects?" I said.

Nurse Lance shrugged. "Beats me. It's never been

administered to a human before." He reached for a needle. "If you're worried, I can easily sedate you."

I backed away. "I'm fine, I'm fine! C'mon, Beep, let's get out of here."

Dazed, I floated out the door. Could this day get any worse?

And that's when I saw the one thing you never, *ever* want to see while you're floating through the hall of a space school: the thin wall between me and space had suddenly disappeared!

The day was officially worse.

SPLOG ENTRY #6:
New and Improved

Beep, look!" I yelled. "We're doomed!"

Beep turned. "Doomed?"

I pointed. "The wall—it's gone! We're about to be sucked into space!"

"Yay!" Beep said.

"Not yay!" I said. But it wasn't too late for action. So I did the one sensible thing I could think of: put my hands over my eyes and screamed!

"Gahhhhhh!" I said. "I can see my own bones!" I lowered my hands. "And I can see inside you, too!"

Beep blushed. "Inside Beep?"

His stomach held a horrible mixture of melted ice and pencils and hot fudge and my favorite red sock I'd been missing since yesterday and . . .

"Beep, did you eat my sock?"

He tried to cover himself. "Sock? Who sock?"

I pointed. "The one right there."

"How Bob-mother see?"

I blinked. "I don't know." And that's when it hit me: "I have X-ray vision! It must be a side effect from that stuff getting in my eyes."

Beep shook his head. "Poor Bob-mother."

I looked through my hand again. "Actually, it's pretty cool. I can see my distal phalanx. My first metacarpal. My scaphoid!"

"Bob-mother make funny names too."

"Those are names of bones, Beep," I explained.

"Bob-mother smart."

"Whoa, Beep. You're right." I could feel a warm tingling all through my head. "The medicine is also affecting my left prefrontal cortex!"

"Huh?"

I grabbed Beep by the shoulders. "This is incredible, Beep. For the first time in my life I actually feel smart. Discerning. Knowledgeable. Sagacious!"

Beep shook his head. "Not self."

"Exactly! It's overriding my fear receptors too. I feel . . . I feel brave!"

Beep clapped. "Very not self!"

"It's amazing, Beep, my chum!"

"What chum?" asked Beep.

"Friend. Comrade. Acquaintance. Pal."

He smiled. "Beep chum!"

"Hurry, let's get back to class. With any luck, Professor Zoome will be giving us a big test!"

We returned just as Lani was finishing her report on our trip.

" . . . and in conclusion," she said, "my pet—I mean *subject*—spiders, Alpha, Beta, and Zilly, enjoyed the trip very much. Or, in their own words . . ." Smiling, she then pulled out a jar, in which the spiders had written in their webs:

Her smile faded. "Some planet," she whispered to Zilly. "You were supposed to write some *planet*."

Zilly scampered sadly down her web. I grabbed the jar and studied her closely.

"It's understandable that Zilly is distracted," I pointed out. "After all, she's carrying 2,128 eggs inside her, which will one day hatch into 2,128 hypercute spiders."

Beep looked at Zilly and clapped. "Spider-mommy!"

Lani's mouth dropped open. "How do you know that, Bob?"

"Um . . . just a guess." I was now smart enough not to advertise my amazing new abilities.

Blaster stepped forward. "Looks like Bob thinks he has *X-ray vision*. Just like LunaGirl!" LunaGirl is a very popular cartoon character of our time. At least with five-year-olds.

I winced as I looked at him. "I thought you liked LunaGirl."

"No way," Blaster said. "She's for girls."

I leaned over to Beep and whispered, "Then why is he wearing LunaGirl underpants?"

Beep clapped. "Bob-mother funny!"

Professor Zoome cleared her throat. "If we could please end our discussions, I'd like everyone to clear their desks. It's time for a big test."

"Yes!" I whispered.

Zenith raised her hand. "What's the test on?"

"Black holes."

"But we haven't even learned about black holes!" said Zenith.

"Of course you haven't," the professor said. "The literature about black holes is unbearably confusing."

Kids started to grumble. How could she test us on something we hadn't studied?

I raised my hand. "What if we actually visited one?"

The room became silent.

"Go on, Bob," she said.

"There's a super massive black hole at the center of the galaxy. It would be a great learning opportunity. As long as we aren't sucked in and crushed into micro-atoms, that is."

I looked around the room. All my classmates seemed terrified. Even Blaster looked faint.

But Professor Zoome clasped her hands and beamed. "Exactly what I was going to propose! Kids, bring an extra-yummy lunch tomorrow for the trip. It may be your last. Class dismissed."

SPLOG ENTRY #7:
Back to (Sigh) Normal

Beep and I made our way toward the dorms. For once, life was looking up. I was smart. I was brave. And because of me, we were actually going to experience the deadliest wonder of nature!

Beep tugged on my sleeve. "Bob-mother? Beep have big question."

"Go ahead, Beep. Ask me anything! The speed

of light. The composition of Saturn's rings. The number of atoms in the universe!"

"What color Beep sock?"

I glanced at his bare feet. "That's your big question?"

He rubbed his tummy. "Beep eat more sock. Fun game."

I sighed. "If you insist." I looked into his tummy. At least, I tried to.

"Well?" Beep said.

"Hmm, let me try again." I squinted. Hard. I could see an inch in, maybe two, but even that was getting difficult.

"Oh no," I said. "The side effects of the spray must be wearing off!"

"Power go bye," Beep said.

I feared he was right. "Let's get back to our room. Quick!"

Before we could move, Lani swooped in. "Hey. I've been looking for you."

"I'm kind of in a hurry," I said.

"And I'm kind of worried," she said. "And not just me, the entire class. No one's ever been to a black hole before. Do you even know what they're like?"

"Well," I said. "By studying the quantum theory of curved space-time, one can deduct that black holes are very, um . . ."

"Dangerous? Hazardous?"

I struggled. "Very, um, very, um . . ."

"Deadly?"

Did she have to keep saying those things? "I meant to say very . . . black."

Beep shook his head. "Sock not black, it *blue*."

Lani looked at me in disbelief. "What's going on with you, Bob?"

I faked a smile. "Nothing. Never been better."

"Anyway, all I'm asking," she said, "is if you know what you've gotten us into?"

"I'd much rather go on a hayride!" I blurted out.

Lani gave me another strange look. "Are you *sure* you're okay, Bob?"

"Uh . . . Uh . . ."

Now that I was my normal self again, my worst fears washed over me. Heights, check. Darkness, check. Space, check. Death, check.

Black holes had them all.

"Gaaaaaaaaaaaaaaaaaaaaaaaaaaaaaah!" I screamed, rushing away.

I was doomed. I was doomed!!

I raced by my classmate Hadron, who was holding his bare foot. "Has anyone seen my blue sock?"

Doomed.

SPLOG ENTRY #8:
The Best of Plans, the Worst of Plans

I lay in bed that night going over possible solutions with Beep, who had the top bunk in our quarters.

"I can pretend to be sick," I said.

"Plan good!" said Beep.

"Of course, then Nurse Lance will insist on giving me a shot."

"Plan bad."

"I know! I'll suggest an even better destination!

We can go to the moon of Mars, the one that has that new candy factory. Everyone likes candy factories."

"Plan good!" said Beep.

"But that's where they take all the kindergarteners. Professor Zoome would never agree."

"Plan bad."

"How about I steal the Astrobus, travel to the outer rings of Saturn, and hide there?"

"Plan good!" said Beep.

"But I don't know how to fly."

"Plan bad."

I thought and thought and thought. Then I dozed a little. Then Beep and I read some comics. Then I dozed some more. Then Beep's snoring woke me up (not to gross you out, but he snores from his *bottom*, if you know what I mean).

I sprang up so hard I came out of my bed-straps

and floated into the middle of the room.

"I got it!" I said.

Beep's eyes popped open. "Plan good?"

"Very good. My problem isn't the black hole. It's my personality! We have to go back to the health office and snatch that bottle of Freeze B Gone. To make me smart and brave again."

"Plan good! Plan good!"

"And when I say *we* I mean *you*."

"Plan bad! Plan bad!"

"No, Beep, it's logical: The spray cures my fears. But I'm scared of Nurse Lance. So I can't get the spray unless I've already *had* the spray."

Beep nodded. "Logic good."

"Plus"—I floated closer to put on the charm—"if you do a good job I just might have an orange-swirl ice pop waiting with your name on it."

"Why Beep want name on it?"

"In *sprinkles*."

"Oooooooooh," Beep said, his face brightening. "Sprinkles good."

"Great." I landed back in bed. "Now let's get some rest. We're going to need it."

The next morning, no one in class seemed very happy. Probably because, thanks to me, we were about to head on a journey with little hope of return.

On the other hand, our lunches were extra yummy.

The second that attendance was done, I raised my hand. "Professor Zoome?"

"Yes, Bob?"

"Before we go, can I take Beep to the health office?"

"Is something wrong?" she asked.

I leaned forward and lowered my voice. "Well, uh, Beep likes to sleep on the bus, and, um, he's been *snoring* a lot lately. Don't want to, you know, stink up the place too bad."

She lifted an eyebrow. "Hurry back."

"We will."

I led Beep to the health room door. "You remember what to do?" I whispered.

He nodded.

"Then go," I said, pushing him inside. I ducked down behind the door to eavesdrop.

"Well, hello there, little one," I heard Nurse Lance say. "What kind of shot may I be giving you today?"

"No shot. Beep swallow sock."

"Ah, I see. So it's surgery you require. I'll get my laser."

"No. Beep want *more* sock."

"But I don't have more socks. Only the ones I'm wearing."

"Look good to Beep."

"Hands off!"

"Beep sad with no sock."

"Here, you can have a bandage roll."

"Yum!" Beep said.

"You weren't supposed to eat it!"

"More?"

"No more!"

"Pencil?"

"Certainly not."

"Cottony ball?"

"Leave those alone!"

"Squirt bottle?"

"Don't open that!" Nurse Lance said. "That's the medicine cabinet!"

I heard crashing. "Oop," Beep said. "Beep sorry. Beep help clean."

"You've been enough help already. Just get out!"

"But Beep want more."

"I said, out!" Nurse Lance yelled.

"Bye!" Beep said as he drifted out.

"And stay out!" As the door slid shut, I heard Nurse Lance's muffled voice add, "Hey, where's my sock?"

I pulled Beep around the corner. "Did you get the spray?" I asked.

He smiled wide.

"Beep, you're my hero!" I glanced at his empty hands. "Uh, where is it?"

"Safe place!"

"Behind your back?" I asked.

"Back no safe, silly Bob-mother."

My heart began to sink. "In your ear, maybe?"

"No in ear!" he said. "That tickle."

I gulped. I didn't want to know. I really didn't. "Safe where, Beep?"

Beep patted his tummy. "Bottle yum!"

SPLOG ENTRY #9
A Tale of Two Tummies

I wanted to be mad at Beep, but he'd done exactly what I'd asked. The problem was, I didn't have a plan B. Or C, or D, or even Z to the 10th power.

All I had was a yummy lunch (jelly but no peanut butter, yes!).

As we floated back to class, we ran into Professor Zoome, who was already leading the others down the hall. "Beep and Bob!" she called. "The Astrobus is leaving in two minutes!"

"But—" I began.

"No buts. We're on a tight schedule."

Suddenly, I had a plan B. "But my lunchbox is in the classroom. I have to go back and get it!"

"No time," she said, dragging me along. "You can have half of my peanut butter sandwich."

"I'm allergic to peanut butter," I said.

"Then you'll just have to hope they have a food court."

"By a black hole?"

"You never know," Professor Zoome replied.

Beep clapped. "Food court!"

I slapped my forehead.

Moments later Beep and I were aboard the bus,

watching a trail of kids slink by us, one by one. It was as if we were invisible. No one wanted to come near us.

"No one like Beep?" Beep asked, his eyes wide with hurt.

"No, Beep. They don't like *me*," I said, looking at the floor.

"Hey, Bob," I heard a voice say. "Mind if we sit here?"

I looked up at Lani and smiled. "Sure."

"Sure you mind or sure we can?"

"Lani sit next to Beep and Bob-mother!" Beep answered.

Unfortunately, Lani clutched her jar of those icky crawly things. Did she have to bring that everywhere?

As it took off, the Astrobus shook, stirred, pushed,

pulled, stretched, and flattened every atom in my body. We swung a hard left at Neptune. And my stomach swung a hard right.

As we passed Pluto, Beep said, "Where ice pop Bob-mother promise?"

How could he even think of eating at a time like this? "Aren't you full of socks?"

"Socks not in *eat*ing tummy."

I looked at him.

"Socks in *pouch* tummy!" To my shock, he reached into a pocket of skin on his front and pulled out a red sock.

"Whoa!" I said. "I didn't know you could do that."

Beep pointed into his mouth. "Go down right side, go to eating tummy. Go down left, go to pouch tummy. Then Beep reach in pouch to take back out."

"I wondered where you always stored stuff," I said.

He patted himself and belched. "Beep pretty full. See, here blue sock," he said, pulling more stuff out of his pouch. "And bandage roll. And green sock. And medicine spray. And yellow sock. And pencil. And—"

"Wait, medicine spray? That's the Freeze B Gone!" I grabbed it before he could swallow it again. "Beep, I could kiss you!" Okay, maybe not kiss. But I did lean over to hug the little guy. Which probably would have been nicer if my arm hadn't gotten stuck in his pouch.

"Tee-hee, tickle!" Beep said.

"Gross! *Gross!*" I said. "Stop squirming, Beep, so I can get it out!"

"Beep tickle! Beep tickle!" he laughed, squirming even more.

Sadly, it went on like that for a while. By the time I finally got free—and Beep stopped giggling—the bus was quiet. Everyone was gaping out the window.

With a growing sense of dread, I turned. "Oh . . . oh no."

Beep peered out too. "Beep no see nothing." He wiped the glass. "Just black."

"Exactly," I whispered. We were there.

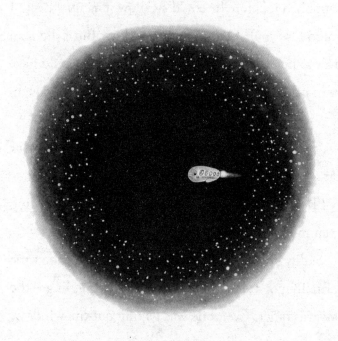

SPLOG ENTRY #10:
Testing, Testing

Warning: I'm about to write a graphic, horrifying splog entry that you might want to skip if you're sensitive to those kinds of things. Sorry, but the part coming up is about to get a bit—last chance to bail, I really did warn you—*educational*.

That's right: As we were all staring into the vast hole in space that was deeper and blacker and more mind crushingly terrifying than anything I'd ever imagined, Professor Zoome decided to give a *lecture*.

"Black holes," she began, "are defined as regions of space-time formed by the death and collapse of very large stars, resulting in compact, dark masses with such strong gravitational fields that nothing that gets caught in their pull—including matter, light, or money—has any hope of ever coming back out. Any questions?"

Hands went up.

"Yes, Comet?"

"Will this be on the test?"

"If you survive, yes."

More hands went up.

"Hadron?" Professor Zoome said.

"What if we *don't* survive?"

"A zero will be averaged into your final grade. Zenith, you have a question?"

"What if we're only injured?" Zenith asked.

"Injuries by black hole are not possible. Once you pass even a micrometer beyond the point known as the 'event horizon'—or *bye-bye forever zone*—you will be stretched into an infinite strand of subatomic spaghetti."

Beep raised his hand. "Ooo, ooo!"

"Yes, Beep?"

"Spaghetti yum!"

"That was not a question. My informational talk is now concluded. Please suit up so you can go outside. Who would like to be first in the air lock?"

Before I knew what was happening, a hand grabbed my arm from behind and thrust it into the air. "Me, me!" Blaster said, mimicking my voice.

Professor Zoome smiled. "Very brave of you, Bob. Once again, very brave, indeed."

SPLOG ENTRY #11
Spaced Out

As I was suiting up, Professor Zoome went over the rules.

"Once you're outside, class, you'll be connected to the bus by a thin rope that attaches to your Emergency Space Pack. Whatever you do, don't push the Quick Release Switch, which is right next to the Self-Destruct Button."

Who designed these things?!

"Please stay with your partner and record as many observations of the black hole as you can. Extra credit to the student who goes closest to the bye-bye forever, *event horizon*—without being sucked inside." She looked at me. "Ready?"

"Al—almost," I stammered. "Just have to, uh, tie my shoe."

"Space boots don't have laces," she pointed out.

"They don't?" I said, kneeling anyway. Then, when I was sure no one was looking, I lifted the spray bottle of Freeze B Gone and doused it all over my head.

"Ready now?" Professor Zoome said.

"Coming. Just need my helmet and I'm set." I grabbed it from the seat, but somehow it didn't feel right. "Wait, this isn't my helmet," I said. "This is a jar of . . . gaaaaaaaaaaaaaaaaaaaaaaaaaaaaaaaaaaaah!"

Lani grabbed the jar of spiders away. "That's not funny. You're scaring them!" She peered inside. "It's okay, Alpha. Don't tremble, Beta. Hey, where's Zilly? Zilly?"

Behind her, Blaster laughed. Well, *some*one thought it was funny.

The spray's side effects must have been kicking in, because I squinted at Blaster and bravely said, "You're a mean bully, you know?"

He held up his hands. "I was just kidding."

"Yeah, sure," I replied.

He suddenly got all serious. "Really. I'm sorry." He held up my actual helmet. "Here, no more jokes, okay?"

I took the helmet. "I guess."

He held out his hand. "We sporky?"

Sporky was *my* word. But I wanted to be a good sport, so I shook. "Sporky."

Next to me, Beep was trembling. "No sporky! No sporky!"

"It's okay, Beep," I told him. "I'm fine now that I have this bottle of . . . Wait, what's this?" For the first time, I read the bottle closely. "Beep, this isn't for brain freeze. It's for *fleas*. You got the wrong spray!"

"Bob-mother no have fleas," Beep said. "It work!"

"Oh no. Oh no."

"Time to go, Bob," Professor Zoome said. "But please don't forget to put your helmet on."

"But . . ."

"Now into the air lock."

"But . . ."

"Attach the thin space rope."

"BUT . . . !"

She pushed a button, thrusting me into raw space, and waved.

"Have fun!"

SPLOG ENTRY #12:
Point Break

Okay, so there I was: my darkest hour. Just me, space, and the gaping mouth of a super massive black hole.

But you know what? As bad as life gets (and it gets pretty bad!), there's one thing that can always make it better: a faithful field trip partner by your side.

That's right: a faithful field trip partner. Right by your . . .

I turned left. "Beep?"

I turned right. *"Beep?"*

I spun around. "BEEP?"

Beep waved from *inside* the safe, warm Astrobus!

"BEEP, GET OUT HERE!" I screamed.

Within seconds the bus door opened and he shot out to join me. "No worry," he said, holding up his thin cord. "Beep bring space rope."

"Did you remember to hook it to the ship?"

His cheeks reddened. "Oop."

"Beep, hold on!" I grabbed on to him before he floated away.

Beep turned toward the vast swirl of infinite darkness. "View nice. Beep draw."

"It's just *black*," I said.

Beep nodded. "Easy that way."

I struggled to keep my grip firm as Beep rummaged in his pouch for his drawing supplies. But my gloves were thick, and I didn't know if I could hold on to Beep for much longer. At least things couldn't get worse.

Then I heard a snap.

"BEEP!" I yelled. "Our space rope just snapped! We're doomed!"

"Doomed!" he yelled back.

"Doomed!" I yelled.

"Doomed!"

"Doomed!"

"Doomed!" I yelled. Or was that him? I was losing track.

Then I just started to scream. "Gaaaaaaaaaaaaaaaaaaaaahhhh!"

"Gaaaaaaaaaaaaaaaaaaaahhhh!" Beep screamed back.

"Gaaaaaaaaaaaaaaaaaaaahhhh!" I screamed.

"Gaaaaaaaaaaaaaaaaaaaahhhh!"

"Gaaaaaaaaaaaaaaaaaaaahhhh!"

"Gaaaaaaaaaaaaaaaaa—wait, who scream now?" Beep said.

"You!"

"Why Beep scream?"

"Our space rope snapped!"

He tugged the taut rope. "Rope no snap."

"It didn't?"

He shook his head sadly. "No. More worse."

"What could possibly be worse than our space rope snapping?!"

He held up his pencil. "Point break."

The pencil point? That was *it*? I wanted to strangle him. But before I could, a voice came on in my helmet: "Professor Zoome here. Bob, are you alive?"

"I think so," I squeaked.

"Good," she answered. "Because the rest of us are suited up and ready to come out. We're just awaiting your word."

That was easy: "*HELP!!!*"

"An odd word for the occasion," she said. "But a word all the same. We'll be right out."

"*LET ME BACK IN! PLEASE LET ME IN!*"

"I only asked for one word, Bob. Please follow directions. Professor Zoome out."

SPLOG ENTRY #13:
Lost and Found

One at a time, students left the bus. Before I could say *Silvery spaceships speed by sparkly stars* five times fast, the entire class was dangling outside at the end of their own very thin space ropes. Beep still held on to mine.

Hadron pointed his camera at the black hole and snapped a few shots, then frowned at the results. "Guess I forgot to turn on the flash."

Professor Zoome smiled at the black hole. "Isn't it simply singular?" At least *she* was having a good time.

Zenith floated up to me. "Hi, cutey," she said.

I reddened. "Uh . . ."

"Not you!" she said. "Beep!"

Beep floated upside down. "Beep cutey! Beep cutey!"

I glanced around. "Where's Lani? Isn't she with you?"

"She's still in the Astrobus," Zenith said. "She lost something important, and she's looking for it."

"C'mon, Beep," I said, aiming us toward the bus window. Sure enough, Lani was floating up and down the aisle, looking under every seat. I knocked on the glass. "Zenith said you lost something," I called. "Can I come in and help you look?"

She faked a weak smile. "That would be great."

"What'd you lose? Your notebook? Your helmet?" I glanced at Beep. "Your *sock*?"

"A zillion times worse!" she cried.

"Your lunch?" I guessed.

She held up that awful jar. "I thought Zilly was hiding, but she must have gotten out! Where could she be? I'll die if she's lost!"

I recoiled. "Well, gee, I hope you find it," I said.

"You're not going to come in and help?" she said.

"It's just that I, you know, have this black hole to explore, and I kind of need all the extra credit I can get, and . . ."

I stopped at the eerie sound of laughter by my side. It was a laugh I knew well.

Blaster's.

I slowly turned. It was Blaster, all right.

"Looking for something?" he said, smothering another chuckle.

Beep tugged on my arm.

"Not me," I said. "Lani. She lost her"—I didn't even want to say it—"arthropod, or whatever you call it."

"Spidey," Beep said.

"Spid-*er*," I corrected him.

"No!" Beep said, pointing wildly at my forehead. "Spidey! *Spidey!*"

Inside the bus, Lani smiled and let out a huge sigh. "Bob, there she is! What a relief. She's been with you the whole time!"

And that's when I felt the light movement on my skin and realized that of all the infinite spots in all of infinite space in all the infinite universes, Lani's creepy spider happened to be in the worst spot imaginable:

MY HELMET!!!!!!!! !!!

SPLOG ENTRY #14:
Bye-Bye Zone

'd like to say that I then found the courage to let the awful, hairy, disgusting creature continue to crawl over me long enough to make it back inside the Astrobus.

But I didn't.

Instead, I clawed at my visor.

And opened it up.

The spider whooshed right out.

Luckily, before all my oxygen could whoosh out with it, I slapped my visor back down.

I sucked in a deep breath. "Whew, that was close, Beep. Unlike you, we Earth beings need to breathe."

He pointed to a little speck in the distance. "Like spidey?"

I watched it float away.

Yes. Like spidey.

"Bob!" Lani called. "Do something!"

I turned to tell her it was too late. And anyway, it was just a spider. But then I saw Lani's face pressed to the window—sad and scared and helpless. Even if she suited up in record time, she would never make it out before her favorite—but, for the record, *disgusting*—pet was sucked toward certain doom. (Along with its 2,128 unborn awful little babies.)

And it was all my fault.

"Bob, please," she pleaded one last time.

I spun toward the others. "Catch it!" I called. "Someone catch that gross little thing!"

Zenith swiped for it. But missed. Flash was speedy. But he missed too.

Hadron was still trying to figure out why his pictures came out so dark.

Professor Zoome zoomed, but even she was too late. The spider was now past the longest space rope. A few thousand more feet and it would be sucked into darkness forever.

Beep tapped my shoulder. "Spidey have to go bye?" he asked. "Like Beep get lost and go bye from Beep family?" Did he really have to tug on my heartstrings like that?

I faced the black hole. Which was certain death.

Then I faced the bus. And Lani.

Then the black hole again. Did I dare attempt the impossible? Without the spray? Could I find my courage after all?

"Oh, *now* I get it," Hadron said, holding up his camera. "I left the *lens* cap on."

SPLOG ENTRY #15:
BIG Trouble

So let's see, what horrible thing happened next? Oh yeah: My space rope tautened and I couldn't go any farther. Even though the rope was my only lifeline to the bus, I reached down and hit the Quick Release Switch. With a click, the rope came free.

Beep was still clinging to me, so I brushed him

free. "Get back to the bus, Beep. Before the strong pull of the black hole sucks you in!"

"Where Bob-mother go?!"

I aimed for the black hole. "I have a plan, Beep."

"Good plan?"

I shrugged. "Probably not."

Before I could stop him, Beep zoomed after me and grabbed on. "Then Beep come too!"

A small part of me wanted to argue with him. But the bigger part was glad he was there.

"Keep your eyes on the spider," I said. Ahead of us, it flailed its little legs. I wondered how much longer it could survive.

"This fun!" Beep said, waving his sketchbook. "Beep draw."

"Beep, this way!" I flew forward, hand extended. The spider seemed to be slowing down. All I had to do now was to carefully reach out, put my hand around its disgusting little body, and . . .

"Got it!"

In front of us, the black hole loomed larger.

"Now what Bob-mother do?"

That was a very good question.

I yanked off my Emergency Space Pack. "There's one last part of my plan, Beep. But I can't make any promises." I pulled out item after item—whistle, Kleenex, sewing kit—and tossed them away. "It has to be in here somewhere."

Beep caught the items with his mouth. "Yum!"

"Here it is!" I said, but it turned out to be the number 2 pencil.

Beep scowled. "No time for draw, Bob-mother."

No kidding! Panicked, I kept searching until, finally, I found it: the Temporary Giganticizer Ray!

Beep clapped. "Make Beep big! Make Beep big! Make Beegib!" Another tongue twister.

"Not you," I said, pointing the ray at the only target that could save us now. "Zilly."

I pushed the button before I could change my mind. In a quick, terrible instant, the inch-long web-crawler in my hand ballooned up to the size of an asteroid. To my infinite horror, I could now count each bristling hair on its slimy body and catch the gleam on the end of each sharp fang.

"Gahhhhhhhhhhhhhhhh!" I said, grasping on to a leg the size of a tree.

"This Bob-mother good plan?" Beep asked.

"Now, Zilly!" I called. "Shoot your web! Shoot it right at the bus!"

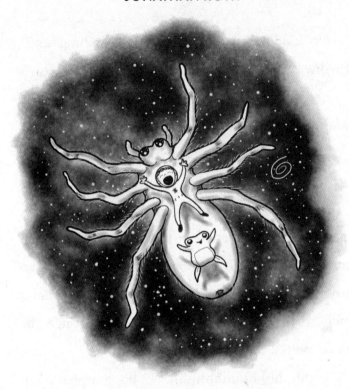

The spider stared at me with multiple rows of gigantic glass eyeballs. They reflected the bus on one side and complete blackness on the other. We whooshed faster and faster as the giant force of nature pulled us in. We were seconds from being stretched into spaghetti and swallowed whole.

"You do understand, Zilly, right?" I said. "It's all up to you now!"

To my horror, the spider then turned to face the black hole straight on.

"Other way, *other way*!" I screamed.

But Zilly didn't budge. She was going in headfirst, and taking us with her.

"Listen, I'm sorry if I offended you, Zilly. Spiders just creep me out, that's all. Nothing personal, right?"

Still nothing. We were doomed.

"Sorry, Beep," I said. "Plan bad. Plan very, very bad."

I closed my eyes and waited for the end.

SPLOG ENTRY #16:
Radiant

Speaking of ends, if I'd ever bothered to actually *learn* about spiders, I would have known that most species shoot their webs from spinnerets—yucky things located on their *bottoms*.

Zilly wasn't turning to face the black hole, she was aiming her web-shooters at the bus.

Good thing too, because about one second from

the point of no return, Zilly shot her webs—*thwap, thwap*—and we were saved.

"Beep says yay!" said Beep.

"Yay!" I yelled.

"Kk-kk!" said Zilly.

Except that—just our luck—the web *missed the bus*!

"Beep says oh no!" said Beep.

"Oh no!" I yelled.

"Kk-kk!" said Zilly.

But then I realized that Zilly's web had stuck to something else: Blaster's helmet! And since he was attached to the bus by his rope, we were now attached too.

"Beep says yay!" said Beep.

"Yay!" I yelled.

"Kk-kk!" said Zilly.

Zilly reeled us in, a split second before the Temporary

Giganticizer Ray wore off. I tumbled through the air lock door as Zilly shrank back to normal size.

"Are you all alive?!" Professor Zoome asked when we were inside.

"I think so," I said. To my side, Blaster scraped web strands off his visor.

Professor Zoome reached around to give me a single pat. "You've earned a passing grade indeed."

Lani was waiting with her jar. "Zilly!" she cried, hugging the small spider.

"Beep hug too?" Beep asked.

"Absolutely," Lani said, hugging him, too.

Then she floated before me. Was I going to get a hug too? Not that I wanted one, because I don't really go for those kinds of things, especially from girls. I was just an ordinary space explorer, doing what needed to be done. In fact, I . . .

. . . felt the air being squeezed right out of me!

"Lani hug Bob-mother!" Beep said. "Lani hug Bob-mother!"

A bright light flashed. "Yes!" Hadron said as the moment was immortalized on his camera. "Finally."

SPLOG ENTRY #17:
Good Night, Space

Good news! Professor Zoome looked at my splog entries so far and told me I got a perfect grade and six stars of extra credit! She also said she looked forward to seeing me write more about my memorable (but horrible) adventures in space.

To which I said: "You know what? Me too!"

"Beep draw! Beep draw!"

"Yes," I told Beep, "you can still do the drawings."

(Until I can afford to hire a professional, that is.)

"Send time-velope now?" Beep asked.

I had put all the entries from the week into one folder, and the folder into the time-velope. I was about to hit send when I heard a knock on my dorm room door.

It was Lani.

"Oh, hey," I said.

"Hey," she replied. "What are you doing?"

"Sending my splogs."

"Then what?"

I shrugged. "No big plans."

"Great." She brightened. "Because I was thinking: How would you like to go check out a comet with me? Or maybe explore the asteroid belt? Or maybe . . ."

"Actually," I said, "Beep and I thought we'd stay in tonight and read comics. It's been a long week. Very long."

"Oh." She bit her lip and floated toward the door.

"You can, you know, join us if you want," I added quickly.

"Lani stay! Lani stay!"

She eyed my vintage collection. "Aren't comics for *little* kids?" she asked.

"Comics are for *everyone*. Here, check one out." I tossed her a title, believe it or not, called *Spider-Man*. I think it was about some awful, evil supervillain. I sure wasn't about to look at it.

She grinned at the cover. "Thanks," she said, her voice bright. "This does look fun."

"Comics, yay!" That was Beep, not me.

"Speaking of spiders," she said, "Alpha, Beta, and Zilly wrote some new things in their webs today. Want to see?"

She'd brought *spiders* to my room?! No offense, but

even though I owed my life to one, spiders still made me cringe.

I gulped. "I guess."

She opened her pack and pulled out the jar. "I think you'll like it," she said.

I got closer. And peered inside.

Alpha's web said $ax^2 + bx + c = 0$. Beta's said *Pi r squared*.

And then there was Zilly's. It said:

I couldn't help but smile. "And you're pretty sporky for a spider, Zilly."

"And Beep!"

"And Beep, too."

And so we curled up with our comics, ate some orange-swirl ice pops, and had a pretty good evening in space.

SEND

Bob's Extra-Credit Fun Space Facts! (Even though nothing is fun about space!)

Pluto was first discovered in 1930 by some guy named **Clyde Tombaugh**. But since it's so small and so far from Earth, not even the biggest telescopes could tell if it was blue or green or yellow like Pluto the cartoon dog. But then the *New Horizons* space probe flew by in 2015, and people everywhere learned that Pluto is rusty orange with a big white heart! It's not a real heart, of course, just a giant skating rink of frozen **nitrogen**, **methane**, and **carbon monoxide**, whatever those things are. Pluto also has five **moons**, which may seem like a lot, but it can get pretty lonely out there.

Though Pluto was once called a **planet**, it was then demoted to a *dwarf* **planet** for some reason, and the kids of Earth were not happy. Kids like Pluto because it's small and cool. An eleven-year-old girl called **Venetia Burney** even got to give Pluto its name! I don't know what it was called before that. Probably **Dwarfy**.

Pluto *is* pretty cool—in fact it's about **minus 380 degrees**! So if you ever go there, remember to *always* wear your Ice Boots and never, ever, ever, EVER try to lick the ground.

ACKNOWLEDGMENTS

It takes a large ground crew to help even a small book series blast off. My amazing crew includes my stellar agent, Natalie Lakosil; my out-of-this-world editor, Amy Cloud; the planet's best writing partners, Fataima Ahmed and Lauren Francis-Sharma; my long-time mission buddies, Robin Galbraith and Kurtis Scaletta; the indispensable communities of SCBWI, the 2017 Debut Group, the Electric Eighteens, and the entire team at Aladdin; my star-bright

ACKNOWLEDGMENTS

sisters, Catherine and Elizabeth, and bro, Matt; my talented niece Gwen (whose artistry can be found in one of the Astrobus windows); my first and most important teachers: my mom, Karen, and dad, Guy; and the one who truly makes me fly, my dear wife, Lisa Marie. To you all, Beep says YAY!

Party Crashers

SPLOG ENTRY #1:
Star Bores

Dear Kids of the Past,

Hi. My name's Bob and I live and go to school in space. That's right, space. Pretty sporky, huh? I'm the new kid this year at Astro Elementary, the only school in orbit around one of the outer planets. There's just one micro little problem:

SPACE IS STUPENDOUSLY BORING!

I mean, sure, you can spend about two minutes

staring out giant picture windows at the infinite wonders of the universe. But then what? We're so far from Earth, the television reception is terrible. And the only channel that does come in well is—don't say I didn't warn you—*educational*.

Beep just said, "Beep like watch *Star Words*! Learn from robot ABCD-2!" Beep is a young alien who got separated from his 600 siblings when they were playing hide-and-seek in some asteroid field. Then he floated around space for a while, until he ended up here. Sad, huh?

You know what's even sadder? I was the one who found him knocking on our space station's air lock door and let him in. Now he thinks I'm his new mother! But since he also thinks *Star Words* is a good show (even though it's for three-year-olds), you can tell he's a little confused.

But I still like him.

"Beep like Bob-mother, too!"

Beep is pretty good at drawing, so I let him do all the pictures for these space logs (splogs, as we call them) before sending them back in time for you to read. Just don't hold me responsible if he only doodles his favorite *Star Words* alpha-bots.

Anyway, that's my life. Enjoy!

SPLOG ENTRY #2:
Party Invites from Heaven

Okay, I know I just said space was pretty much the most boring thing ever, but that was *before* I had to sit through our class history reports. Each student had to choose a book about a historical event and report back to the class.

After listening to Zenith drone on about the first moon missions, and Blaster share every detail about World War P, I didn't think there was any history *left*. My brain was seconds from shutting down.

"Very good, children," Professor Zoome said when they were done. "Sadly, we don't have time for more today. We will resume on Monday with"—she checked her clipboard—"Bob."

Beep clapped. "Bob-mother, yay!"

Gulp. I wasn't even halfway through the book I'd picked out yet! I leaned toward Beep and whispered, "Luckily, she didn't say *which* Monday."

"And by Monday," she continued, "I mean the day after the day after tomorrow."

Beep clapped again. So much for a nice, quiet weekend staring out the window.

Lani grabbed my arm when I was halfway out the classroom door. Lani (short for Laniakea Supercluster) is my best friend at school who *isn't* a confused alien. Not that I think about her a lot or anything, but "Lani" means "heaven" in Hawaiian. Of course, "Lani" can also mean "sky," depending on—

"Hey, Beep! Hi, Bob! I'm glad I caught you," she said. "Are you doing anything this weekend?"

My face grew hot. "Well . . . ," I began.

"Great!" She pulled out a couple of envelopes. "Because I'm inviting you both to my birthday party!"

Birthday party? I broke into a cold sweat. "There's not going to be a clown, is there?"

She shook her head. "No. Why?"

"My parents hired a clown for my birthday once, and I had to hide in a closet the whole time."

Lani smiled. "No clown, Bob. I promise."

"Whew. But, uh, what about

a magician? Because there was this other incident—"

"No magician either."

"Swell. And no guy in a purple dinosaur suit?"

"Bob, how many traumatic birthdays have you had?"

I counted on both hands. "Pretty much all of them."

"Well, this one's going to be different," she said. "Just be sure to bring a bathing suit."

"You're having a pool party?"

"There's a pool in the water park."

I perked up. "Water park?"

"Actually, where we're going, there are three water parks."

"*Three* water parks?"

"But if those aren't your style, there are also sixteen amusement parks."

"Sixteen amusement parks!"

"Though, if that's too tiring," she said, "I suppose you could stay in your room and surf the twelve million hypershow channels."

I began to drool. "Tw-tw-twelve million?"

"It's a lot, I know," Lani said. "But my parents insisted on having the party on some amazing new star cruiser that's taking a tour around Neptune. I hope you don't mind."

I shook my head. "We can handle it."

"I'm so glad!" Lani said. "We leave tomorrow and get back Sunday night."

Beep pulled on my sleeve. "When Bob-mother do big report?"

I pushed him away. "Silly Beep! He's always

joking." But when Lani was gone, I added, "Don't worry, Beep. I'm sure I can fit in my homework somewhere in between SIXTEEN AWESOME AMUSEMENT PARKS!"

I tore open the invitation. It read:

Lani is having a party!

On the maiden voyage of

the STARSHIP TITANIC!

Motto: The 100% Safest Ship in the Galaxy.

100% Guaranteed!

"Hmm, that name sounds familiar," I said, reaching into my backpack for the book I chose for my report (mainly because it was the only history book in graphic novel form I could find). It was about some ship that sailed on Earth a really long time ago (even for you kids of the past).

I read the title: *Titanic: A Night to Remember.*

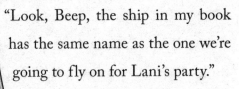

"Look, Beep, the ship in my book has the same name as the one we're going to fly on for Lani's party."

"How book end?" Beep asked.

I shrugged. "I haven't gotten that far yet. Frankly, even history *comics* are kind of dull." I shoved the book back into my pack.

"What if end bad? *Starship* end bad too?"

"Don't be silly, Beep. It's the 'One Hundred Percent Safest Ship in the Galaxy. One Hundred Percent Guaranteed!' Even *I* won't be nervous about rocketing around space for a change."

Beep clapped. "Bob-mother no scared!"

"Yep! For the first time in my life, Beep, I think it's all going to end just fine."

SPLOG ENTRY #3:
All Present

We were supposed to be packed and ready for the voyage by noon Saturday, but I was so excited that I woke extra early: 11:49.

I unstrapped myself from my bed, floated out from the sheets, and called to the top bunk, "Wake up, Beep, we have to go!"

But his bed was empty. "Beep?" I spun to see him sitting at his desk.

"What are you doing?" I said. "Homework?"

"Beep watch *Star Words*!"

On screen, C-345 was teaching ABCD-2 the correct way to spell A-S-T-E-R-O-I-D. I gave Beep a once-over. "Have you been watching that all morning?" I asked. His eyes had that orange glaze that appears when he doesn't sleep for at least eleven hours.

"Plus night," Beep admitted.

I pushed the off button. "We're going on an overnight trip. We have to pack." I began shoving stuff in my backpack. "Bathing suit, check. Toothbrush, check. Pack of gum, check. Extra underwear, check. Extra pair of socks, check."

"Socks, yum!" Beep said, pointing to his tummy.

I sighed. "Make that *ten* extra pairs of socks." Soon my backpack was bulging. "So why does it feel like I'm forgetting something?"

"More sock?"

"No, something else." I scanned the room. "Well, I guess it can't be all that important."

Beep patted his pouch (when Beep eats something, it either goes into his eating tummy or his pouch tummy). "Beep have all need here."

"Then we're off!"

《 ∗ 《 ✪ 》 ∗ 》

Sadly we had to take the Astrobus (motto: 100% *Smell*iest Ship in the Galaxy) to get from school to the *Starship Titanic*.

Lani was waiting by the bus door. "There you are, Bob. I was worried you weren't going to make it on time. Everyone else is already here."

"Sorry. Just making sure I packed enough socks."

She studied my backpack and smiled. "Looks like there must be something more than just *socks* in there."

"No, pretty much just socks." I rolled my eyes. "Beep eats them by the dozen."

"Socks yum!" Beep said.

Lani winked. "Okay, Bob, *socks*. I'll take your word for it."

"What else would I have in here?" I asked as Beep and I floated aboard the bus.

Before she could answer, I froze. Lani's other friends were already seated . . . with big, fancy wrapped gifts on their laps!

"Oooh, pretty," Beep said, fawning over all the sparkly bows and ribbons.

I slouched into my seat and strapped myself in. "Uh, Beep," I whispered as the Astrobus took off. "You didn't happen to buy Lani a birthday present, did you?"

"What that?"

"Something you get someone to show how much you care about her."

"What Bob-mother get Lani?"

"Well, that's the problem," I admitted.

Beep gasped. "Bob-mother bad!"

"Hey, you didn't get her anything either."

Beep's eyes welled with tears. "Beep bad too!"

"No, Beep, shh, it's fine," I said. "You didn't know."

Beep nodded. "Sometimes good not know."

"Tell me about it," I agreed.

"Bob-mother not know lot of things."

"Well, I wouldn't say—"

"Bob-mother know *any*thing?"

"I know I have to find a good gift, Beep. And fast." I rummaged in my pack. "She told me once she likes gum."

Beep reached into his pouch. "Beep have pencil!"

"I doubt that's enough."

He broke it in half. "Two pencil?"

"Uh . . ."

He put it back. "Beep keep thinking."

I unwrapped a piece of gum and sank into my seat. "Bob-mother too."

But my thoughts were soon interrupted by a chorus of oohing and aahing. Beep pulled my sleeve. "We there!"

I straightened to look out the window. "Whoa," I said, shielding my eyes. "If that's the *Starship Titanic*, it's as bright as the sun."

"That *is* sun," Beep said, and spun me around to the window on the opposite side.

"Whoa!" I said, shielding my eyes even more. The massive star cruiser loomed before us like a floating city of lights. "Beep, have you ever seen such a sight?"

"Ooh! Aah!" Beep answered, but then I realized he was watching the video screen on the seat back in front of him. "ABCD-2 yay!"

I grabbed my backpack. "Beep, we're docking. And you're about to have your choice of twelve million *real* channels. Let's go!"

SPLOG ENTRY #4:
Gravity Falls

One of the ship's stewards—another word for really fancy helpers—met us as we floated onto the deck of the *Starship Titanic*. "Watch your step," he said.

I winked. "Good one," I said to him, because there are no "steps" in space; the zero gravity thing takes care of that! We float *everywhere*.

Then I tripped over my feet and crashed into the floor.

"WHEEEE!" Beep said, doing the same.

"Need some help?" Lani asked. She gripped my hand and pulled me up.

"You didn't tell me they had gravity here," I said. Gravity is super expensive in space, so the ship had to be high-end.

"My parents say this ship has everything," Lani said.

"Yeah, like something for super rich people," I said. "I'm sure glad our tickets are free."

"Speaking of my parents, there they are!" Lani said. "Mom, Dad, over here!"

"Uh, the tickets *are* free, right?" I said.

Lani didn't answer me as her parents approached, trailing a line of stewards who carried their luggage.

Each steward gripped a suitcase in each hand and tucked a bag under each arm. I bet *they* weren't super happy about all this gravity, since it makes objects heavier!

"Laniakea, darling, how nice to see you," her mother said.

Lani gestured to the bunch of us. "Mom, Dad, these are my friends: Beep and Bob and Zenith and Flash and Andromeda and the rest."

Her parents shook our hands. "Pleased to meet you, Beep and Bob and Zenith and Flash and Andromeda and the rest."

Her father snapped his fingers, and a dozen more stewards appeared. "Please take our guests' belongings and escort them to their cabins."

Lani reddened. "It's okay. We don't mind carrying our own things."

But one steward had already taken my backpack, and another picked up Beep.

"Wait, he's not luggage!" I said.

"Is too!" Beep said, and whistled as the steward carried him along.

Lani walked next to me as the group followed the steward to our rooms. "Sorry about that. My parents are, well, used to having people do things for them."

"Cool!" I said.

"Sometimes," she said. "But just because we have help doesn't mean I think I'm better than anyone."

"So your parents have money?" I asked.

Zenith, on the other side of me, whispered, "Bob, you dolt. Lani's parents are the owners of Supercluster Industries!"

"What's that?"

Zenith rolled her eyes. "Only one of the biggest companies in the solar system."

"Wow," I whispered, and then I started to put it all together. "Hey, Lani," I said, "did you know your parents are *rich*?"

She stared ahead. "Perhaps."

"I mean, *really* rich."

"Perhaps!"

The steward stopped and turned to me. "This is your room, sir."

"I'm a *sir*?" I said.

"Yes, sir."

Beep jumped out of his arms. "Beep sir too! Beep sir too!"

"Yes, sir."

The steward opened the door and led us inside.

"The room is equipped with the finest amenities in seven dimensions, but if you should need anything else, please push this red button and I will be back to assist."

Beep pushed the button.

"Yes, sir?" the steward said.

"Beep need hug."

"Yes, sir," the steward said, bending to put his arms around Beep.

"Now Beep need carry to bed."

"Certainly, sir."

"That's okay," I said. "Beep can walk."

Beep pointed across the wide room. "But bed far."

The steward handed Beep a remote control. "This will bring the bed to *you*, sir."

Beep pushed a button and the bed began to hover. Beep clapped and jumped on.

"Will that be all, sir?"

"Yes, thank you," I replied. Then I said good-bye to Lani and the others, who left to find their own rooms.

The second they were gone, Beep began to fly his bed in circles. "WHEEEE!"

"Could you stop that, Beep? I'm dizzy just watching you."

"Then no watch!" he said, switching to figure eights. He was pretty good with that thing.

"I'm going to unpack," I said, heading toward the dresser.

Just as I was stashing away the last of my socks, there was a knock at the door. It was Lani and the rest of the group. "Uh, hate to interrupt the fun, but want to go have some more fun?" she said. "We're heading to the rides!"

"Sure, let me catch Beep, and we'll meet you there."

"We'll be at the Super Nova Infinity Drop, Bob. See you soon!"

I waved at Beep. "Beep, c'mon. Get down so we can go." But he had found the video clicker, and suddenly a giant hyperscreen appeared in the room. "Oh, no, not *Star Words*."

Beep clicked to a shopping channel, where they were advertising precious stones. "That good birthday present for Lani-friend! Beep buy?"

"Not now, Beep."

"Now?"

I knew I had to buy Lani a gift, but it could wait. "Sheesh, Beep, we'll have plenty of time to buy her something later. Don't you want to go on some rides?"

Beep jumped off the bed, then pushed the red button. Within moments the steward appeared again.

"Yes, sir?"

"Beep want hug bye."

"Certainly, sir."

And then we were off.

SPLOG ENTRY #5:
Ups and Downs

The amusement parks took up a massive section of the star cruiser's enormous domed deck. I studied a map inside the gate. "Right now we're at the baby park. But each park gets more fun until"—I zoomed in—"the Super Nova Infinity Drop!"

"Ooh," Beep said.

"Ooh is right. It says the ride is so fast it actually

warps through time. One ride only takes seconds, but seems like three hours."

"Aah!"

Truthfully, it sounded a little scary. "Of course, Beep, if there's *another* ride you want to go on first . . ."

Beep pointed and took off in a flash. "There!"

I ran to keep up. "But that's a *little* kid ride."

Beep didn't care. "Balloon Blast! Balloon Blast!" he said, reading the sign.

A bored-looking man in charge of the ride said, "Each of you sit on one of those chairs. Then I'll tie on just enough balloons so you can float."

"What's fun about this, Beep?" I asked. "We float all the time."

"Not with balloon!"

After we sat, the man entered the number 15 on

some machine called a Balloon-o-Matic, pushed a button, and fifteen floating balloons on strings suddenly appeared. He tied them to my seat and studied Beep. "You'll need about thirty."

"Beep want billion!"

"That would be enough to lift this entire ship!" the man said.

Beep clapped. "Yay!"

The man gave Beep an annoyed look. "You get thirty. And here's a needle; don't lose it. Next!"

Once the man let our chairs go, we began to float up, up, up, and . . .

"Beep, we're only about five feet off the ground," I said.

Beep glanced down. "Oooooh. Aaaaaah."

A girl who looked like she was four years old floated past me and stuck out her tongue. Off in the distance, the Super Nova Infinity Drop flashed like a beacon of *real* fun.

"This is lame, Beep. Let's get off." I waved at the man below. "Excuse me, but we're ready to get down."

"That's why I gave you a needle, kid!" he shouted back. "Just reach up and pop."

I tensed. "But . . . but I don't like popping balloons!"

The man shrugged. "Welcome to my world."

"Bob-mother scared of pop?" Beep said.

"Not *scared*," I said. "Just a weensy bit terrified. You see, it all began at one of my early birthday parties. The one with the, you know, *clown*."

"Beep not scared!" Beep said, reaching up to a balloon with his needle. I flinched at the sudden explosion. He lowered by a foot or two. "Now Bob-mother turn."

I lifted the sharp needle toward the closest balloon. An inch away. A half inch away. A half a half inch away. A half a half a half . . .

"Bob-mother take long time," Beep said.

"Don't rush me!" I said. "Okay, here goes." The needle pressed into the balloon. But nothing happened. I pushed a little harder. Still nothing.

"Uh, I think this needle might not be sharp enough," I called down to the man.

"Or maybe you're not strong enough!" he called back. The four-year-old floated past me and stuck out her tongue again.

"Here, Beep help," Beep said, grabbing my foot

and yanking until we were even again. He pointed his needle at one of my balloons.

"No, wait, Beep, I . . . AHHH!" I said at the sudden sound.

"One pop for Bob-mother!" Beep said. "One pop for Beep! One pop for Bob-mother! One pop for Beep!" And so on, for what felt like an endless descent. But finally, we made it.

I crawled off the seat, trembling, just as Lani and the others came ambling by.

"Bob, there you are!" Lani said. "I thought you were going to join us at the Super Nova Infinity Drop. It was transdimensional!"

"Sorry. Got carried away."

"On a baby ride?" she said.

I pointed to the sign. "Technically, you have to be at least three."

"Well, glad you liked it, Bob. But dinner and birthday cake are in half an hour. Promise you won't miss that, right?"

I patted my stomach. "Are you kidding? I wouldn't miss dinner for anything!"

Lani smiled. "Great. Wear your best suit. And see you then!"

SPLOG ENTRY #6:
Not Suited for This

Since it took less than a minute to change, and only twenty-five to nap off the excitement of the balloon ride, I was a whole minute early to dinner. (See, I could be on time after all!)

A man in a tuxedo gave me a funny look, then opened the door to the ballroom. "This way, sir."

I leaned toward Beep. "I'm kind of getting to like all this sir stuff."

"Ooh," Beep said, blinking at sparkling chandeliers that dangled over round, white clothed tables as far as the eye could see.

I saw Lani sitting down and headed to her table. "Well, we made it," I announced.

Lani looked at me and froze. "Bob, are you wearing a bathing suit?!"

"My best one." I gulped. "Isn't that what you said?"

"I meant best *formal* suit. This is a luxury star cruiser. Did you really think we were eating poolside?!"

Beep hid his towel behind his back.

Lani heard her name being called and hissed, "My parents are coming! Please, Bob, try to make a good impression."

Beep reached into his pouch and pulled out a red button.

"Where'd you get that?" I said.

He jabbed it frantically. "Yank off wall."

"Beep, it's not going to work now that it's—" Before I could finish, our friendly steward appeared by our side.

"Does the young gentleman require a jacket?" he asked, slipping one over my shoulders.

"Uh, thanks," I said, stepping behind a chair so Lani's parents wouldn't notice my bare legs. And just in time.

"Mom, Dad," Lani said, "you remember all my friends."

"Of course," her mom said, nodding to the circle of us around the big table. "Good evening, Beep and Bob and Zenith and Flash and Andromeda and the rest. Don't you all look delightful. Please, take your seats."

"Thank you," we all said, except for Flash, whose tie was so tight it looked like he might pass out. I kind of hoped he did, so I could steal his pants. Lani sat on one side of me and Beep on the other.

A waiter wearing a hat was walking by our table. I waved to him. "Excuse me, can we get a couple cheeseburgers here?"

Lani's mother gasped. "Young man, that is no way to address the ship's captain!"

"C-captain?" I stammered.

He turned my way, and I braced myself for a stern lecture. But instead he bowed and said, "Captain Smith, at your service."

"Oh, in that case," I said, "do you also have fries?"

The captain stroked his beard and laughed. "You have a bold sense of humor, son."

Beep clapped. "Beep want fries too!"

"He likes orange ketchup," I added. "But only if you have it."

"We have everything you can imagine on the *Starship Titanic*," the captain said with a smile. But his face then darkened. "Except escape pods, of course. Those were deemed unnecessary for the One Hundred Percent Safest Ship in the Galaxy."

Flash blanched. "No escape pods! But what if we hit something?"

Captain Smith shrugged. "Eh."

Lani's father stood. "Thank you for gracing us with your presence," he said to the captain. "But I'm sure you have more important tasks to attend to."

"Not really," the captain said. "Computers pretty much run this thing. I spend most of my day on the Super Nova Infinity Drop." He sighed. "Even the ride operators get to push more buttons than I do."

An attendant tugged on the captain's sleeve. "Sir, we are approaching Neptune. You are needed right away."

The captain brightened. "To pilot the ship?"

"To dine with the Neptunian Countess. She just arrived."

The captain hung his head. "Oh." He then made his way to a big table in the center of the room.

"Ooh, look," Zenith said, "here comes the countess now. Isn't she elegant?"

"She's blue," I pointed out.

Beep, who's also blue, clapped.

"What's that sparkly, purple heart-shaped thing on her chest?" I asked.

"That sparkly *thing*," Lani said, "is the most valuable jewel in the solar system: the Heart of Neptune!"

"Yum!" Beep said.

"Not for eating!" I said.

Lani smiled. "Isn't it simply exquisite?"

Then it hit me: I still hadn't found Lani a gift! What was I supposed to do now? I began to push myself away from the table. "Uh, I think I have to go. . . ."

"Dinner is served!" a steward announced, and at once waiters appeared carrying trays.

"Your meal, sir," one said, putting a plate in front of me. "Does the gentleman require anything else?"

Just a perfect, thoughtful birthday present for a super rich girl who probably already owns her own moon. I slumped in my seat. "No, I'm fine."

"Excellent," he said.

But really, I was doomed.

SPLOG ENTRY #7:
This Spells T-R-O-U-B-L-E

After a hearty dinner Lani turned to me and said, "Isn't this exciting? Soon we'll be orbiting Neptune."

"But we go to school by Saturn," I pointed out. "And Saturn has all those pretty rings."

"Neptune has rings too," she said. "I mean, they may not be as big or well known as Saturn's, but they're still very interesting. The first of the five major rings is made primarily of large ice chunks—"

I braced myself for one of her long science lectures. Luckily, her mother interrupted: "Laniakea, it's almost time for cake. And you're not going to want to miss your *special* surprise."

"Yes, Mom." She leaned toward Beep and me and added, "Don't laugh, but she always has my cake served by costumed TV characters I *used* to think were cool when I was little. It's so embarrassing."

"As long as it's not a clown," I joked, "I'm fine."

Lani smiled.

"Or a magician," I added. "Or a purple dinosaur. Or a—"

"Okay, Bob, we get it."

Out of the corner of my eye, I could see a couple stewards begin to wheel in a table stacked high with wrapped gifts. Ugh. Then the lights suddenly dimmed.

PARTY CRASHERS

"Hey, look," Flash said, pointing across the room. "Is that who I think it is?"

All attention went toward a pair of robots: one tall and golden, the other short and round. The large one carried a cake with flickering candles.

"Oh no," I said.

"My rusty circuits may be mistaken," the larger robot said as he headed our way, "but I do believe we have a birthday girl in the audience."

The little robot spelled, "B-I-R-T-H-D-A-Y. Birthday!"

Beep gasped. "That be . . . that be . . . that be . . . *ABCD-2*! From *Star Words*!" He began to bounce, but I held him down.

In the dim lighting the little alpha-bot kept bumping into people at their seats as he rolled by. Including the Countess!

"Oh dear. I do apologize for his clumsiness," the tall robot, C-345, said.

Lani's mother beamed. "Laniakea, it looks like your favorite *stars* are here."

Lani, reddening, whispered to me, "Yeah, from when I was three."

I struggled to keep Beep from leaping out of his seat. "Well, at least *some*one's excited."

Beep clapped. "ABCD-2! ABCD-2!" Then he jumped from his chair right onto the poor robot, sending him to the floor with a crash.

As I tried to pry Beep off, a panel opened near the top of the ABCD-2 costume. "Hey, buddy," the guy inside said, "you're ruining our gig. Help me up, will you?"

"Sorry about that," I said, struggling with Beep to lift ABCD-2. For a guy in a small costume, he was surprisingly heavy.

C-345 put the cake in front of Lani and said, "Birthdays are F-U-N, fun, children, because we can practice our numbers. How many candles can we count? I see one. I see two. I see three. . . ."

Before he could finish, Lani leaned forward and

blew. The candles went out and everyone clapped.

"Time to spell the birthday song!" C-345 said, and began to sing one letter at a time: "H-A-P-P-Y B-I-R-T-H-D-A-Y T-O Y-O-U! H-A-P-P-Y B-I-R-T-H-D-A-Y T-O . . ."

When he was finally (finally) done, a small cake carving knife came out of ABCD-2 (I could see the guy's hand—it wasn't the most convincing costume ever).

"And with that," C-345 said as the lights came back on, "my little counterpart and I must now say our good-byes. That's G-O-O-D-B-Y-E, good-bye."

When he realized what was happening, Beep leaped forward and clutched ABCD-2 in a tight embrace. "No go! No go!"

A shriek split the room before the robot could reply. Everyone froze.

"My diamond bracelet!" someone screamed. "It's gone!"

"My heirloom watch!" someone cried. "It's gone too!"

Everyone began to look down. Lani's mother gasped. "My wedding ring!"

"My earrings!"

"My pants!" (That one was me.)

But the greatest cry came from the center of the room, where the Countess of Neptune was frantically clutching at her chest . . . for the priceless Heart of Neptune that was no longer there!

SPLOG ENTRY #8:
Exposed!

Within seconds a band of burly security guards burst onto the scene. The doors closed and locked as someone shouted, "NO ONE IS TO LEAVE THIS ROOM!"

Beep held tightly on to ABCD-2. "Bad happen! Beep scared! Want cake!"

I tried to pry him off. "You can't have cake until you let go of this robot. You're crushing the poor guy inside."

"Guy inside?!" Beep unclenched, and the robot rolled quickly away.

"Everyone, freeze!" A woman in a sleek black uniform stepped forward. She tapped her badge. "I am Chief Trappz, head of ship security. I will be in charge of this investigation. If you have any questions, too bad, because I'll be the one asking questions. Isn't this awesome?"

Beep clapped, and the chief shot him a look. Then she came closer. "First question," she said, pointing toward our table. "What flavor is that frosting?"

Lani raised her hand. "Excuse me, but what does frosting have to do with finding the Heart of Neptune?"

Chief Trappz narrowed her eyes. "Did it occur to you, miss, that in the thief's panic at being discovered, they dropped the jewel into the cake, with the intent of later claiming the piece with the indented frosting for themselves, thereby committing the perfect crime?"

"Really?" Lani said.

The chief scooped some frosting up with her finger. "Nah, probably not. I just like frosting." She popped it in her mouth, then summoned her guards with a snap. "We'll start our interrogation here. Check them all."

Lani's mother stood in protest. "But they're just children!"

"Exactly," the chief said. "The least suspicious is always *most* guilty."

"Really?"

Chief Trappz shrugged. "I watch a lot of movies." She then noticed the gift table. "What's inside those boxes, miss?"

"I don't know," Lani said. "Could be anything."

The chief raised her finger. "Exactly! Squad, start there."

Before Lani could stop them, the guards began to rip open her presents. One held up a long tube.

Zenith smiled. "That's from me. It's a time-o-scope. For looking back in time!"

"Keep searching!" the chief barked.

"Uh, actually," I said, "that thing might be good for finding the crook. All you have to do is look back about ten minutes in time and—"

The chief held up her hand. "Excuse me, but this is *my* investigation. And I don't use toys, I use my *wits*. Next gift box, please."

Another guard held up a small device with an arrow.

"Ooh, that's from me," Andromeda said.

Lani smiled. "A Matter Detector. You can program in any substance and it will point to it. I've always wanted one! Thanks."

Andromeda reddened. "I know you like boring science things."

"Uh, forgive me for pointing this out," I said to Chief Trappz, "but I bet if you programmed that matter finder thing for *jewels*, it would—"

"Enough!" she said. "Next."

As Lani watched, the guards opened everything. And big surprise, no Heart of Neptune anywhere.

The chief sighed. "I suppose I have to move on to the next table." Finally!

Lani raised her hand. "Excuse me, but are you sure those were *all* of the gifts?"

"It's probably best not to bother the chief," I whispered.

"But, Bob," Lani said. "I haven't seen *your* gift yet. You're a good friend, so I know it must be special."

I felt every eye in the room upon me.

"Well?" Zenith said. "Do you have a gift for her or not?"

"Of course he has something," Lani said. "Bob is always so thoughtful."

"Then, where is it?"

I could feel my heart pounding. How was I going to get out of this one? It was too late to buy her anything. I didn't even know how to fold cool napkin animals. No, even though it would be hard, there was probably only one sure solution: the truth.

"I . . . I got you something super special," I said, "but then a black hole formed and my gift fell inside, and so I went back to the gift shop but some aliens attacked and stole all my money, and so all I had left was some gum to give you, but then . . . then . . . then . . ."

The look in her eyes told me I was doomed. There was only one thing left to do. I spun and pointed. "Beep didn't get you anything either!"

The crowd gasped. "Beep, is that true?" Lani asked.

Beep jumped. "No true! No true!" He pulled half a pencil out of his pouch and smiled.

"That's your present?"

"And *this*!" Beep said, pulling out the other half. But when Lani didn't smile, Beep said, "Wait, must be even more." He fished around in his pouch. "Hmm, what this?"

"Seriously, Beep," Lani said, "you don't have to—"

"Ta-da!" Beep said, pulling out a new find. "Beep get special shiny just for you!"

But Lani, along with everyone else, only gasped at the enormous purple jewel in Beep's hand.

The Heart of Neptune!

SPLOG ENTRY #9:
An Arresting Development

could hardly believe what I was seeing. Beep, the sweetest little alien ever, would never steal. It was impossible!

Then again, that valuable heart-shaped rock *was* in his hand.

Chief Trappz folded her arms. "I rest my case. Guards, arrest the guilty party."

Beep clapped. "Party, yay! Now cake?" But his

happiness turned to confusion when the guards bound his arms behind him.

"Wait!" I said. "Beep is innocent! He was never properly taught right from wrong."

The chief huffed. "So you're saying we should arrest his *parents*?"

I nodded. "Exactly."

"Fine. Where are they?"

"Well, that's hard to say, because—"

Beep pointed at me. "Bob-mother Beep mother! Bob-mother Beep mother!"

The chief rolled her eyes. "Cuff him, too."

As they led us away, I tried to catch Lani's eyes. But the second I did, she glanced down.

"Lani-friend no like shiny?" Beep said to me.

"Not if it belongs to the Neptunian Countess!"

Beep hung his head. "Beep only try make happy."

"I know you did," I said. "But people aren't happy with gifts you *steal*."

"Beep no steal!" he said. "Beep find."

"Yeah. In your *pouch*. Which doesn't exactly look very good. The main question is, how did it get there?"

Beep shrugged. "Fall from space?"

"Not very likely," I said.

"Beep eat by mistake?"

"Possible, I guess."

"Bob-mother put there?"

"Not me!" I said. "But I think you may be on the right track. Like Chief Trappz said, the real thief must have panicked when they learned we were all about to be searched. So they got near enough to plant it on you. But who?"

And then it hit me. I turned to the guards. "Wait!

Stop! I know who stole the Heart of Neptune! And all the other stuff too."

"Tell it to the judge," a guard replied as he halted us in front of an open door.

"Is this"—I gulped—"the ship's jail?"

The guard leaned closer and grinned. "Worse. These are your *quarters*."

I looked inside. "Hey, Beep, he's right. This is our room! Well, that's not so bad. We still have over twelve million channels and—"

"Your quarters," the guard went on, "with all the electronics turned *off*!"

"Wait, what? You mean no TV? No video games? No Internet? No—"

"No nothing!" he said. He uncuffed us and shoved us inside.

SPLOG ENTRY #10:
That Sinking Feeling

WARNING: The next entry is going to be very grim. Please skip ahead if you are sensitive to terrible situations—in this case a boy and his friend being deprived of the most basic of kids' rights: lots of glowing screens!

"Beep, this is bad," I said after what felt like ages. "Without something to watch, I'm starting to actually hear my own thoughts. I don't know how much more I can take. How long have we been in here?"

Beep pulled his watch out of his pouch. "Minute."

"There's nothing to do! I'm lost in a fog. I have to get out of here!"

"Now *two* minute."

I took a deep breath. "There must be some kind of entertainment here. Think, Beep, think."

He pointed to the large picture window. Outside, the spectacular view of Neptune filled the frame. "Planet pretty!"

"Maybe if I just pretend it's a movie," I said. I sat

on the floor. "See, it's almost like a giant screen." But within seconds I could feel myself fidget. "Beep, nothing's happening. It's just a big, beautiful, scenic wonder!"

He pointed. "Ooh, Neptune do have rings. Tasty blue!"

I squinted at the thin bands encircling the planet. They grew larger as we approached, but that was about it.

"Sorry, Beep, but I think I'm going to die from boredom now. It was nice knowing you."

"Nice know Bob-mother, too. Beep have Bob-mother gum when gone?"

I clutched my backpack. "No, you cannot have my gum!"

"When Beep have cake?"

I gently put my hand on his shoulder. "Beep, I

don't know how to break this to you—but I don't think they're going to give us any."

His eyes began to well with tears. "Beep sad!"

"Oh, don't cry, Beep. Here, you can have my gum. Take it all."

He reached into my backpack. "This gum big. But Beep eat anyway."

"Wait, Beep, that's not gum." I grabbed it away. "This is a *book*. For my history assignment on that big famous ship that sailed across the ocean." I opened it eagerly. "Can you see how desperate I am, Beep? I'm actually excited to *read*. Now, where was I?"

I flipped to the middle. Luckily, there were lots of pictures. "Here's where I left off: 'The great steamship *Titanic* was only days into its voyage when the unthinkable happened: It hit an iceberg and began to sink.' Wait, what?"

I flipped ahead, narrating the key moments: "Unsinkable ship takes on more water; then more water; then *more* water; and soon it sinks completely into the sea. Beep, this is horrible!"

Beep's eyes welled again. "Story end sad!"

I slammed it shut. "Who knew that history had a *bad* side? Luckily, nothing like that can ever happen again, though, right?"

"But this ship name *Titanic* too," Beep said.

"Yeah, but this one is one hundred percent *safe*."

"Other *Titanic* safe too."

"Yeah, but that one hit an *ice*berg." I folded my arms. "And lucky for us, Beep, there are no icebergs in space."

Beep turned to the window. "No, but ice *ring*."

I spun. "Huh?"

Beep clapped. "Pretty blue ring *big* now!"

The rings of Neptune were big . . . and getting bigger. I realized that we were on a collision course headed straight for them! And with the captain and everyone else in the ballroom, we were the only ones who knew.

So, with certain disaster imminent, I did what I do best:

"GAAAAAAAAAAAAAAAAAAAAAAAA AAAAHHH!"

SPLOG ENTRY #11:
Five Icy Rings

WARNING: If you skipped the last splog entry because of how grim I said it was going to be, you may want to skip back, because things are about to get *much* worse. Or maybe skip back two entries. That would be even safer.

On the other hand, two splogs ago is when Beep got caught with the jewel. And that's what started this whole mess! So you may want to skip back even farther. Maybe to the balloon ride part. The Balloon Blast is a ride for four-year-olds, but it's pretty much the best thing that's happened to me this entire trip. Pretty sad, huh? Who writes these things?

Oh, wait, *I* do.

"And Beep draw!" Beep said, holding up a pencil half. (Then he ate it.)

I dared to glance out the window. While planetary rings may look all pretty and smooth from a distance, up close they're really just an asteroidlike field of giant flying ice cubes.

"AHHH!" I shrieked as one ice boulder hit the glass.

"Ooooh!" Beep said.

"AHHH!" I shrieked as another one hit.

"Ooooh!"

I banged on the door. "LET US OUT! LET US OUT! WE'RE GETTING *PULVERIZED*!"

A muffled voice of one of the guards answered, "Not likely. You're just trying to trick us into letting you go."

"No, I swear! The ship is heading directly into one of Neptune's rings!"

"Nice try, kid. But you're thinking of *Saturn*."

"Go to a window!" I said. "Neptune has rings too!"

"Yeah, sure it does."

I repeated what Lani had told me earlier: "They

may not be as big or well known as Saturn's, but they're still very interesting. The first of the five major rings is made primarily of large ice chunks—"

"Yawn, kid. We're going for a coffee break."

"NO, WAIT!" But they were gone.

I spun. "Beep, we have to do something! Beep? Where are you?"

Then a mattress passed over my head and I ducked.

"WHEEEEEEEE!" Beep said from the flying bed. So I guess they hadn't turned *everything* off.

"Beep, get down from there!"

He landed the bed. "But fly fun."

"There's a time for fun, Beep, and a time for thinking of ways to get out of life threatening situations. You know what time *this* is, Beep?"

He pulled out his watch. "Twenty o'clock?"

"Time to think of a plan!"

Beep touched his chin and put on his best thinking look, but it was too late.

"Oh no!" I said as the glass was pummeled again and the sound of cracking grew. "THE WINDOW'S ABOUT TO *BLOOOOOOOOOW!*"

SPLOG ENTRY #12:
The Good, the Bad, and the Smelly

Good news! When the glass shattered, all the tiny shards didn't shoot in toward me and Beep, like I feared, but whooshed out into space.

Bad news! All the air whooshed out too.

Good news! Just before I got whooshed out with everything else, Beep swooped down on the flying bed and pulled me aboard.

Bad news: The bed then got whooshed out as well.

Good news!: Beep can breathe in space without a space suit.

Bad news: I can't.

Good news!: Now that I knew how my history book ended, I could give my presentation on Monday.

Bad news: I'd never make it to Monday!

Good news!: Just as I was about to pass out, Beep did something super smart, and shoved my entire head into his pouch, which still had air in it.

Bad news: His pouch smells like socks.

Good news!: Beep was a total expert at flying the bed and zipped it all the way to one of the ship's air lock doors.

Bad news: My head was still in his pouch.

Good news!: Beep got us back inside the ship again, where I could breathe.

Bad news: Everything *still* smelled like socks.

I hacked. "Beep, thanks for saving my life and all," I said, "but have you ever considered washing that thing out?"

Beep pouted. "Beep no like bath."

"Well, you're lucky, then, Beep, because there's no time for a bath. We have to get back to the ballroom. Now!"

We ran through the halls, burst through the doors, and raced to our table. "Lani!" I said. "It's okay, Beep and I are alive. But you should have seen what we went through."

"I did," she said.

"What do you mean?"

She held up her phone. "One of the passengers on the upper deck caught you on video. See?" She showed me footage of Beep flying the bed out in space, with my head stuck in his pouch. "It's only been posted on the intergalactic Internet for ten minutes, yet it's already a big hit!"

The number of hysterical laughing face emojis below the video was up to five trillion.

"Oh, great," I said.

Lani hushed me. "Shhh. The captain's making an announcement."

"Good news!" the captain said. "The *Starship Titanic* has now cleared the rings of Neptune. We will not sustain any more damage."

People cheered.

"Bad news," he continued. "Many windows were broken, as well as some large screen TVs."

The crowd murmured.

"Good news!" he went on. "Those are all easily repairable."

People cheered.

"Bad news," he said. "The main thrusters have also been damaged, and thus the ship is unable to fly."

The crowd murmured.

"Good news!" the captain said. "The band is ready to play for this evening's entertainment."

People clapped.

"Bad news," he said. "Without the thrusters, the

ship will plummet hopelessly toward the giant planet below, and since there are no escape pods on board, tonight's entertainment will be the last you ever hear. Please enjoy!"

SPLOG ENTRY #13:
Beep Blow Big Blue Bubble

Within moments the room erupted in panic. People screamed and ran. I could barely even hear the music.

Beep sat calmly at the table.

"Beep, why aren't you freaking out like everyone else?!" I asked.

"Beep wait for cake."

I eyed all the crumb filled plates. "Looks like they already ate it all."

Beep's eyes widened. "Cake gone?"

"Cake gone."

"NOOOOOOOOOOO!" he cried, joining the rest of the pandemonium.

"Here," I said to distract him. "Have some gum."

"Pepperminty, yum!" Beep said.

I popped the last piece in my own mouth, mainly to try to get rid of the sock smell.

Across from us, Lani's father grabbed the captain. "There must be some way you can save us!"

"Lift this enormous ship from the gravitational pull of a planet?" the captain said. "I'm a pilot, not a miracle worker. And not even much of a pilot anymore."

"Then we demand a refund."

The captain pointed. "The refund line's over there."

I turned to Beep. "This is hopeless. What are we going to do?"

Beep blew a blue bubble with his gum and clapped. But his clap popped the bubble, so he had to start again.

"Beep, you're forgetting what I told you about life threatening situation time."

He pouted.

"Now, think hard, Beep, because we—wait, that's it. You're a genius!"

"Beep genius?"

I grabbed his arm. "Quick, this way!"

We passed Lani, who said, "Where are you going, Bob?"

I lifted a finger high. "To the amusement park!"

"Really, Bob? Really?"

"It's not what you think—"

"No, go ahead," she said. "Have your fun."

I kept running. "No time to explain!"

We passed a window, and I tried not to peek at the looming planet below. If my plan didn't work, it wouldn't be long until we went zooming smack into its atmosphere.

I panted as we ran. The bummer about gravity was it made you have to exercise. "Up these stairs, Beep. I think"—*pant*—"we're almost there."

And then, suddenly, there it was: the gate to the amusement parks! Luckily, no one was there. We ran inside. Right up to the . . .

"Balloon Blast!" Beep said. He sat on a chair.

I pulled him off. "Not yet. First, we have to lift the Balloon-o-Matic. And get it to the—I forget what you call the front of a ship. Oh, wait, now I remember: bow."

Beep bowed.

"No, that's the official name for the front of a ship: bow."

Beep bowed again.

"Just help me pick it up!"

We struggled to lift the machine. That was another problem with gravity: It made things heavy. Just as we were getting a good grip on the machine though, a voice boomed from behind.

"STOP RIGHT THERE!"

I spun to see Chief Trappz and her guards.

"Oh, am I glad to see you," I said. "We could really use some help lifting this to the bow."

Beep bowed, dropping his side of the machine.

The chief put her hands on her waist. "Caught you thieves red-handed this time."

"What? No," I said. "We're not thieves!"

"You're stealing that balloon-making thing right before my eyes!"

"Yes, but for a very good reason!" I argued.

She pulled out two pairs of handcuffs. "Tell it to the judge."

The rest of the guards surrounded us. It was no use resisting. I held up my hands. "I guess we have to know when to quit, Beep." I turned. "Beep?"

Before I knew what was happening, Beep grabbed me tight and we, along with the Balloon-o-Matic, were lifted up into the air. Using his alien wits, Beep had programmed the Balloon-o-Matic to make hundreds of balloons to carry us away!

The guards shouted and jumped to catch us and the Balloon-o-Matic. But we were too high.

"Beep!" I said. "You really are a genius."

Beep bowed.

"Now, get us to the bo—front of the ship, Beep. And get ready to make *history*!"

SPLOG ENTRY #14:
Captain Courageous

Good news! We lost the guards and found a small air lock door at the bow of the ship!

Bad news: Beep suddenly needed a bathroom break.

Good news!: After his break, Beep went through the air lock so he could tie a billion balloons to the railing!

Bad news: He forgot to take the Balloon-o-Matic out with him.

Good news!: He came back inside to get it!

Bad news: He remembered he forgot to wash his hands and went back to the bathroom.

Good news!: Beep came back from the bathroom, took the Balloon-o-Matic out through the air lock, set it for a billion balloons, pushed the button, and finally saved the day!

When he was back inside for good, I brushed my hands together. "Well, I'd say we *tied* that problem into a pretty neat knot, huh, Beep? Get it? *Tied!*"

Beep clapped. "Yay tied!" Then he shrugged. "What mean 'tied'?"

"Tied. Like with a string. Like how you *tied* the balloons to the ship." I froze. "You did *tie* the balloons to the ship, didn't you?"

Beep pinched his chin. "Hmmm . . ."

I glanced out the hatch, at the balloons' strings that were floating up . . . up . . . up.

"GET BACK OUT THERE, BEEP! HURRY!"

"But Beep forgot wash hands again."

"Why would you need to wash your hands again?!"

"Beep touch balloon. And kids touch balloon too. Yech."

"They didn't touch *those* balloons."

Beep clapped. "That good. Beep go tie now!"

Luckily, he caught them just in time. And *tied* them until they held. The strings tightened, and the *Starship Titanic* began to lift away from the planet. (Note: Even though balloons don't technically work in space, because space doesn't have an atmosphere, these were special *space gas* balloons. Just go with it.)

When Beep was safely back inside, I collapsed. "Whew, that was close. But we're big heroes now, Beep!"

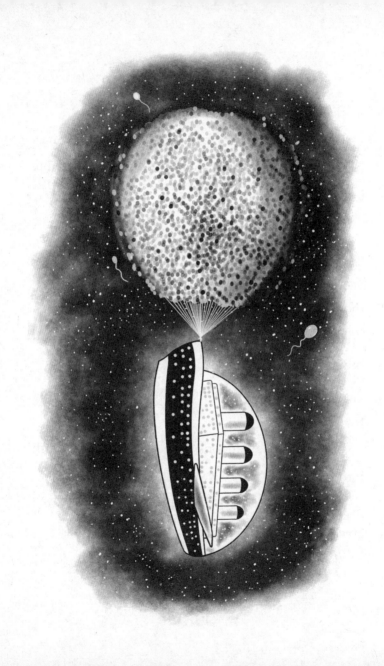

Beep clapped. "Hero!"

I turned at the sound of voices. "Look, here comes Lani, the captain, and the whole gang now. Probably to give us some medals and stuff."

"Bob," Lani said, running up, "what have you done?!"

I folded my arms. "Saved the day, I'd say."

She pointed. "And I'd say we're about to collide with those rings again! Untie the balloons or we'll all die!"

She was right. The ship was headed right toward the icy rings!

"But without the balloons," I said, "we'll crash into the planet!"

"But with the balloons," she argued, "we'll crash into the rings!"

"But without the balloons," I countered, "we'll crash into the planet!"

"But with the balloons—"

Luckily, Captain Smith interrupted: "Stop, both of you! There's only one way to survive. And that's if someone expertly steers the ship through the narrow rings until we are free!" He glanced around. "By any chance, can anyone here do that?"

"Uh, *you're* the captain," I said.

"Yes," he said, "but the computer does all the *actual* navigating. And when it saw what danger we were in, it turned itself off!"

"Can't you call tech support?" I said. "I'm sure this ship has it!"

He held up his phone. "I did, but I'm on hold!"

My panic was renewed. "We're never going to make it!"

"Wait!" Lani said to the captain. "Surely you must have piloted a ship back when you weren't so ancient?"

He stroked his white beard. "When I was a wee

lad, I played with holo-ships in the virtual bath. But those were simpler times."

Beep shuddered. "Beep hate bath!"

"Please, Captain Smith," Lani said. "You at least have to try!"

The captain looked ahead, and a fire began to burn in his eyes. "You're right. I am the captain. I can do this!" He spun. "To the wheelhouse I go!"

The rings loomed ever closer as we waited for the captain to get to the wheelhouse.

"Brace yourself, Beep!" I said.

The rings came closer. And closer. And so close the uppermost balloons began to pop!

"We're not going to make it!" I said.

"No, look, we're veering left!" Lani pointed out.

"Then right!" I said.

Lani stumbled. "Then left again!"

I grabbed hold of a chair. "Then a little jog to the right!"

"Beep too tired for jog," he said.

"Then left and . . . we made it!"

Everyone cheered.

"Thank you, thank you," the captain said as he came back down. He dabbed his eyes. "Guess I am a real captain after all."

Lani smiled. "Guess that's that."

I wiped my brow. "Finally. I mean, this was like one of those horrible movies where you think it's over about twenty times, but there's always one last—"

"EVERYONE RUN!" someone shouted. "WE'RE ABOUT TO CRASH INTO TRITON, THE LARGEST OF NEPTUNE'S FOURTEEN MOONS!"

"Uh, be right back," Captain Smith said.

And then, with one more *big* swerve to the left, that truly was that.

SPLOG ENTRY #15:
And the Band Finally Stopped

The birthday party group and many other guests gathered back in the ballroom to celebrate. The band was still playing.

"How noble," the captain said to the musicians at the end of their song. "You played on even as the ship plummeted to certain doom."

The musicians looked up in confusion.

"Wait!"

"Huh?"

"What?"

The captain then came to our table. "I just want to thank you all for encouraging me," he said. "After what the other Captain Smith, my ancestor from long ago, did to the original *Titanic*, I have now cleared my family name."

I pulled out my history book. "Hey, I know about that! But if you knew about it too, then why did you give this ship the same name?"

He shrugged. "Probably not the best idea."

"I don't suppose," I said, "that you can come to my class on Monday and help me with my history report?"

The captain beamed. "I'd be honored, son. I can talk for *hours* about the *Titanic*!"

"Uh, hours?" I said.

He put his arms around me and Beep. "It's the least I can do for two heroes."

The Neptunian Countess stood. "JUST ONE MOMENT," she said, pointing to us. "Aren't you forgetting that those two are *thieves*?!"

Oh, yeah, that. "No, wait!" I said. "Beep and I are innocent. But I know who the real thieves are. And they're right here in this room!"

Everyone gasped. Chief Trappz and her guards burst into the room.

"Don't worry, they won't escape now!" the chief said, blocking the doors.

"Thief where?!" Beep said. "Thief where?!"

I sighed. "Sorry, Beep, but you're not going to like this. The ones who stole the Heart of Neptune and all the other stuff, and then tried to frame you, are right"—I spun and pointed toward the stage—"there!"

The musicians froze.

"Wait!"

"Huh?"

"What?"

"No, not you!" I said to the musicians. "*Next* to the stage. Quick, they're getting away!"

"Get them!" Chief Trappz commanded.

Within seconds, they were surrounded.

Beep ran to ABCD-2. "Say no so! Say no so!"

A panel on the small robot slid open. And a metal utensil popped out!

"Look out, Beep!" I cried. "He has an ice cream scoop!"

Another panel on the costume slid open, revealing a face. "It was a perfect plan!" he said. "In this costume I could *bump* into anyone, and then snatch and hide the jewels inside! But when I saw they were looking for the big heart-shaped one, I knew I had to dump it. And what better place than the pouch of the little alien who was giving me a hug? We would have gotten away with it too, if it weren't for you meddling kids!"

C-345 kicked the small robot. "Way to admit our crimes, Frank."

ABCD-2 held the scoop higher. "There's still time to escape! And no one can stop us!"

"Oh yeah?" Beep said, and began to jab his red button.

The steward appeared. "You called, sir?"

Beep pointed at the robots. "They need jacket!"

"Of course," the steward said. "One for you"—he draped C-345's head in a tuxedo—"and one for you," he added, smothering ABCD-2 and knocking him to the floor.

ABCD-2's top popped off, and the rest of the

stolen jewels spilled out. The guards pounced in for the arrest.

The steward turned to Beep. "And the new cake you ordered will be out momentarily, sir."

Beep opened his arms. "Happy hug!"

"Of course, sir."

The captain folded his arms. "The stewards here really are top-notch."

"Only the best for my daughter on her birthday," Lani's mother said.

"Birthday!" I said, suddenly remembering. I turned to Lani and hung my head. "Lani, I'm really sorry that I never got you a birthday present. And then sorry I lied about it. And then sorry—"

"Bob, it's okay," Lani said with a smile. "You and Beep caught the crooks and kind of helped save the ship. And most of all, you came to my party. And that's the best gift a girl can have. Well, short of an interdimensional pony."

"Happy hug!" Beep said again, this time to Lani.

The steward lifted Beep into Lani's embrace.

Luckily, I'm not the type who needs that kind of affection. Lani's thanks were reward enough, and, like the captain, I was content to stand tall and—

To my surprise, the steward then lifted me up and plopped me into Lani's open arms too.

And Bob thought, "Yay."

SPLOG ENTRY #16:
A Night to Remember

After Beep ate most of the giant new cake, and Lani's parents and the captain began to drink coffee and gab, Lani suggested we go off for one last fun activity before bedtime.

Beep clapped. "Balloon Blast, Balloon Blast!"

"We stole that one, Beep," I said. "Remember?"

Beep pouted. "Now Beep do."

"Don't worry," Lani said, "I know something even better!"

I crossed my fingers and thought, *Super Nova Infinity Drop, Super Nova Infinity Drop, Super Nova Infinity Drop.* After all I'd been through today, I finally felt brave enough to try it.

I shrugged. "You mean, like the, uh—what's that one called? Oh, yeah, the Super Nova Infinity Something?"

"Drop," Lani said. "Actually, I was thinking more of a stroll along the top deck. Under the stars."

"Uh—stroll?" I said, wondering if I had heard her right. "Under *stars*?"

She lifted her foot. "It feels good to actually walk for a change, instead of float, don't you think?"

Beep shook his head. "Beep like flying bed!"

I had to admit, after hours of all this gravity, I was getting a little tired of using my legs again too.

Lani smiled. "You can't say no to a birthday girl, now, can you?"

"Uh, no," I said. "I mean yes. I mean . . ."

Lani took off, and since there really was no arguing, Beep and I followed.

And you know what?

We walked along the deck, and we talked about silly things, and we peered up at the stars as they flickered down upon the great *Starship Titanic*. And it was totally nice and boring.

Just like I like it.

SEND

Bob's Extra-Credit Fun Space Facts! (Even though nothing is fun about space!)

Neptune is the eighth planet from the sun. It was discovered by astronomers in 1846, but they didn't find it with telescopes—they found it using **math**! (Guess math has some uses after all. Who knew?)

More than a hundred years later they also discovered that Neptune has five major **rings** around it, made of floating ice chunks the size of Texas,

THOUGH NO ONE EVER BELIEVES THIS UNTIL YOU'RE ABOUT TO RUN INTO THE RINGS, AND EVEN THEN THEY STILL THINK YOU'RE TALKING ABOUT **SATURN**! Neptune is also a pretty shade of blue.

Neptune was named after the **Roman** god of the sea, whose name was **Neptune**. Neptune was also the god of horses, but that doesn't make much sense, because horses live on land. Speaking of horses, once at this fair my little sister and I went on a pony ride. My sister was mad because I got a pony with a unicorn horn and she didn't. I knew it was a pretend horn, but I still thought it was pretty cool.

Anyway, that's what I know about Neptune.

ACKNOWLEDGMENTS

The author would like to thank NASA for use of their photographs as source material.

Take Us to Your Sugar

SPLOG ENTRY #1:
Send Snacks!

Dear Kids of the Past,

Hi. My name's Bob and I live and go to school in space. That's right, space. Pretty sporky, huh? Only a hundred Earth kids are picked to go to Astro Elementary each year, and I was one of them. There's just one micro little problem:

THE FOOD!

I mean, they have the technology to make anything, but the only pizza toppings in our cafeteria are broccoli bits and proton sprinkles!

Beep just said, "Sprinkles, yum!" Beep is a young alien who got separated from his 600 siblings when they were playing hide-and-seek in some asteroid field. Then he floated around space for a while, until he ended up here. Sad, huh?

You know what's even sadder? I was the one who found him knocking on our space station's air lock door and let him in. Now he thinks I'm his new mother! Obviously, Beep can be very confused (especially about food, since he *tastes* with his eyes). But I still like him.

"Beep like Bob-mother, too!"

Beep is pretty good at drawing, so I let him do all the pictures for these space logs (splogs, as we call them). Unfortunately, his pencils are yellow, so he thinks they taste like banana. It's not even snack time, and he's already gone through a dozen!

Anyway, that's my life. Enjoy!

SPLOG ENTRY #2:
A Broken Part

I probably shouldn't have spent so much of the last entry talking about food, because now all I can think about is lunch. To make things worse, Professor Zoome has been telling us about a planet covered with volcanoes that spew hot fudge.

"I'd give anything for some hot fudge," I whispered to Beep. "Anything!"

Beep pouted. "Even give Beep?"

"No, not you, Beep."

He smiled.

"I mean, unless," I added, "it was a whole *lot* of hot fudge."

Lani turned from the seat next to me. Lani, short for Laniakea Supercluster, is supersmart, supercool, and superfun (and possibly super*cute*, not that I notice that kind of thing). "Beep is worth way more than hot fudge," she said. "Even if you poured it on the biggest banana split on Saturn."

"Oooh, banana," Beep said, and gulped down the last of his pencils.

When the lunch

bell finally rang, we all shot out of there. "About time," I said. "I'm famished."

"Even after that huge stack of fiberjacks they gave us for breakfast?" Lani asked.

"I only ate the syrup."

Lani made a face. "What about last night's protein patties?"

"I only licked the ketchup."

"Do you eat anything, Bob, that's actually *good* for you?"

"Sure. I had two slices of blueberry cheesecake for dessert." I folded my arms. "Blueberry is fruit."

Beep clapped. "Blueberry, yay!" Blue is one of his favorites.

We floated around a corner and grabbed the railings that led to the cafeteria, which is the one place in our school that has gravity. Gravity is super pricey in space, but it's really hard to keep food on your tray without it. Not to mention chocolate milk.

Mr. Da Vinci, the school's maintenance man, eyed us as we entered. I squirmed uncomfortably. (Okay, so I may have had a major chocolate milk spill recently.)

"Hey, Mr. Da Vinci," I said.

He glared.

"Sorry again about the milk," I said. (Did I mention it was a whole tray? With cartons for my entire class?)

Mr. Da Vinci leaned on his mop and sighed. "All my incredible genius, wasted on the carelessness of children."

I pulled Beep up to the Servo-server. Today's lunch was peanut butter and jelly slabwiches, green matter number B, chocolate milk (no thanks!), and non-astronaut ice cream.

I deleted everything but the jelly and the ice cream.

"I'm allergic to peanuts!" I said to Lani when she shot me a look.

The Servo-server made some cranking sounds and then squirted my order onto my tray. I was particularly excited about *non*-astronaut ice cream for a change. It wasn't even dry and powdery!

Beep waddled next to me. (When he walks, he looks like a penguin.) "Where Beep and Bob-mother sit?" he asked.

This was always tricky. Astro Elementary is full of cliques. The Kids Who Love Math. The Kids Who Really, Really Love Math. The Kids Who Want to Marry Math. And so on.

Me, I'm more of a Kid Who Loves Naps. I like to sit in the back, where you can lean against the wall.

"There," I said, pointing to a table at the far end of the room. "Quick, while it's empty." If I spread out enough, I could even lie down. And no offense to Beep, but he makes a pretty good cushion.

Beep eyed his peanut butter slabwich, then tossed it into his mouth whole.

"You should chew," I said.

"Chew gross," he said.

I put a dab of jelly on my ice cream. "Nothing gross about this. Watch me savor every last drop of goodness."

I shoved a large spoonful into my mouth. "Mmm, mmm," I began to hum, but then I made a very startling and horrific discovery: The ice cream tasted . . . *bad*.

While my throat was already saying, *Swallow*, my brain was saying, *Don't!* With one hack, a stream of jelly and cream spewed out of my nose.

Beep shook his head. "Bob-mother *super* gross."

Of course it was at just that moment that Lani, accompanied by her friend Zenith, chose to join us. Zenith's butt never even hit the seat. "There goes my appetite for a week," she muttered, and spun to leave.

"Bob!" Lani said.

I grabbed a handful of napkins. "It's not"—I hacked again—"not my fault! It's the ice cream and jelly. They're"—I shuddered at the horror—"*not sweet!*"

She took a taste from her own tray. "Blech, you're right. Something must be broken."

A quick glance at the sparks coming off the Servo-server confirmed it. I rushed to Mr. Da Vinci. "There's an emergency! You have to do something! Quick!"

His eyes lit up. "Do you need me to build a device that can control every atom within all six trillion overlapping universes? Because, happily, I'm nearly finished with one!"

There were six trillion universes? "Uh, actually, the Servo-server is on the fritz."

He sighed. "Let me get my tools." He opened the machine and removed a blackened part. "And here we find the problem. The artificial sweetenizer is kaput!"

I froze. In space, it can be very bad when things break. Such as when you're floating in the void, and your oxygen tank gets pierced by a micro-meteor. Or when you're getting ready for bed, and your hyper-toothbrush leaks nuclear plasma.

But none of that comes close to the horror of losing the artificial sweetenizer! *Sweet was my life!* My hands were already shaking from withdrawal.

I grabbed his sleeve. "Tell me you can fix it!"

"Of course I can fix it." He stroked his bushy white beard. "Just have to tinker a bit."

"Will it be done by dinner?!"

"Not a problem, young man. I do my best work in the afternoon."

I let out a sigh. "I guess I can wait that long."

"I'm certain I'll have it by two, maybe three o'clock at the latest." He nodded. "Yes, three o'clock. Of the first Thursday next May."

SPLOG ENTRY #3:
Scream for No Ice Cream

They say in space, no one can hear you scream. But I think that applies only to *outdoor* space, which is a soundless vacuum.

I collapsed onto our lunch table. "Did you hear him, Beep? This is unthinkable. Everything will be unsweetened until next *May*!"

Beep put his arm on my back. "Not so bad, Bob-mother."

"Easy for you to say. As long as your food is colorful, you're fine. But what about me? Do you know how many days it is to next May?" I began to count on my fingers. Tomorrow was September 30, minus the leap year, carry the Tuesday. "Nine thousand!" I said.

Lani rolled her eyes. "Two hundred and fourteen days until Thursday, May first," she said. She was definitely the math-marrying kind.

"When it comes to going without sugar," I admitted, "I'm not sure I can even last another two hundred and fourteen *minutes*."

"Relax, Bob," Lani said. "It could be worse."

"Oh yeah. How?"

"Well, um"—she thought for a moment and then lifted a finger—"the sun could go supernova." Supernovas are when stars collapse into themselves and then explode, vaporizing everything.

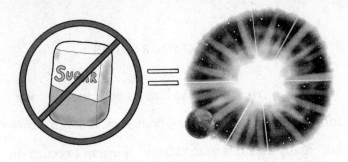

I slumped. "About the same."

"Don't worry," she said. "There's always another solution."

I brightened. "Like asking Principal Quark for a new sweetenizer?"

Lani shuddered. "The last kid who asked the principal for something is still cleaning the plumbing tubes on the outside of the station."

I held up my trembling hands. "See, this is why I always hid a big bag of trick-or-treat candy under my bed back on Earth. For emergencies just like . . . Wait. That's it! Halloween is only"—I calculated on my fingers—"four days away!"

"Actually, thirty-one," Lani said.

I really needed a better math tutor.

"What be Halloween?" Beep asked.

"Halloween," I explained, "is a magical time, Beep. When children dress as monsters and go door-to-door collecting giant bagfuls of free candy." I could feel a tear welling up at the thought of it. "It's the most wonderful day of the year."

Beep's eyes widened. "Bob-mother be monster?"

"Just for pretend, Beep. Or I could dress as a ghost. Or an alien."

"Bob-mother already alien."

"No, Beep. *You're* the alien."

"Beep *alien*?!"

I sighed. "We've gone over this."

He began to bounce and flap his arms. "Beep not alien! Beep not alien!"

"Fine, Beep. You're *not* an alien."

"Beep want meet other not alien," he said. "Other Beeps."

"There aren't any other Beeps here."

"No Beeps?" he said, his eyes filling with tears. I quickly tossed him a pencil. He swallowed it whole.

"You better?" I asked.

"Beep better."

"You know what?" I said. "I'm better too. Even though we've been struck by an unspeakable tragedy, I think I can summon the will to survive another month. Then I'll simply collect enough sweets to last for six years, and that should get me through June."

"Uh, Bob?" Lani said. "Remember when I said it could be worse?"

"What?"

"Promise me you won't scream?"

"Yes, yes, I promise."

"Good. Because, as much as you like Halloween, I think you should know that—well, I'm not sure how far it goes back, at least before I started here . . ."

"Just say it!!"

"Bob." She looked into my eyes. "In space, there *is* no Halloween."

Everything went black.

SPLOG ENTRY #4:
Serious Club Arguments
Really End Sadly

I wish I could say I woke to find it had all been a horrible dream. But as my eyes opened upon a circle of kids (and Beep) staring down at me, I knew it was all too real.

"It's okay, everyone," Lani said. "He's alive."

The crowd immediately lost interest and backed away. Lani held out her hand. "Do you need to go to the nurse?"

I flinched at the mention of Nurse Lance. "No, no! I'm fine. I'm not even seeing little yellow flashing spots on the ceiling."

Lani looked up. "But there *are* little yellow flashing spots on the ceiling."

I squinted. "Really?"

She helped me to my seat. "You don't have to go to the nurse if you promise not to faint again."

"I promise."

"Good. Because, as I was saying, you can't count on Halloween to solve your sugar problems, because we don't celebrate it here."

"GAAAAHHHHHHHHHHHH!"

"Bob, you promised you wouldn't scream!"

"Okay, okay. So why can't we have Halloween?"

"Principal Quark has a strict policy against celebrating *any* planetary-based holidays."

★ 241 ★

"But that's no fair! There must be something we can do."

"Well," Lani said, "we can always gather a group of students and come up with a reasonable list of demands."

"I meant, like time travel."

"I like my plan better," she said.

No one ever likes time travel.

Lani leaned in close. "We should act fast. Gather some kids who believe in the cause and meet me in my room after school."

"But I like to nap after school."

"Bob, do you want to take back Halloween or what?"

I raised a fist. "Or what!"

"Great, you're in charge of snacks. See you there!"

« * « ★ » * »

At exactly 3:05, Beep and I knocked on Lani's dorm room door. I wasn't crazy about missing a nap, but without my normal sugar crash, I actually wasn't all that tired.

She peered down the hall, then let us in. "Bob, I told you to bring others."

"I brought Beep."

"Okay, then, Beep," she said, "who did *you* bring?"

"Beep bring Flash," he said.

"I don't see Flash."

"Beep lose Flash," he said with a pout.

"How can you *lose* Flash?"

Beep shrugged. "Happen fast."

"Well, at least I got Zenith and Hadron to come," Lani said. "Hope that will be enough."

We floated into a circle. Lani raised a small gavel. "I hereby begin the first meeting of the secret club known as S.C.A.R.E.S."

"S.C.A.R.E.S.?" I asked.

Lani smiled. "It's a clever acronym I came up with: Scary Costumes Are the Right of Every Student!"

Beep backed away. "Beep no like scary."

"But it's about Halloween," Lani said.

"I thought it was about free treats," I said, then thought for a second. "Maybe S.C.A.R.E.S. should stand for the Society of Candy Addicts who Rely on Energy from Sugar."

"Good one, Bob," Hadron said, and we high-fived.

"As the president and founder of S.C.A.R.E.S., I say this is not up for discussion!" Lani said. "We're

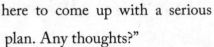

here to come up with a serious plan. Any thoughts?"

Beep waved. "Beep president too?"

"There's only one president,"

Lani said. Beep pouted. "Fine, you can be *vice* president, Beep."

Zenith gasped. "Hey, you said *I* could be vice president!"

"I said I'd *think* about it," Lani said.

"Well, then I *think* I'm going to leave," Zenith said, and huffed away.

"The vice president has no real power!" Lani called after her.

"Beep power no real?" Beep said.

"Only if I die," Lani said.

Beep clapped. "Yay die!"

"Wait," Hadron said. "Who said anything about *dying*?"

"No one's going to die," Lani said. "The worst thing that's going to happen is that we won't make it out of Principal Quark's office alive."

Hadron spun for the door. "I just remembered. I have chess club on Tuesday."

"Today's Wednesday."

The door swished open. "Bye!"

Lani banged the table with her gavel. "Even though S.C.A.R.E.S. is down to just the three of us, I still think we can do this."

"Uh, do what exactly?" I asked.

"March into Principal Quark's office first thing

in the morning to demand our rights!" She pushed us toward the door. "So you better rest up. You'll need all your strength and more if she decides to punish us. See you both then!"

SPLOG ENTRY #5:
Principal's Principles

Between my fear of Principal Quark and my greater fear of no candy, I hardly slept a wink. I was still in pajamas when I heard a knock at our door the next morning.

"Beep! Bob! Wake up!" Lani called. "Time to go."

"Coming," I groaned, and got dressed.

We floated down the hall. "Have you given

thought to what you're going to say to the principal?" Lani asked.

"I have to say something?!" I asked.

"Beep give thought," Beep said.

Lani smiled. "That's wonderful, Beep."

"About club secret shake," he said, and held out his arm. "Go up, up, down, round."

I took hold of his hand and tried to follow along. "Up, down, up, around?"

"Up, *up*, down, round."

"Guys, we're here!" Lani said.

We entered the front office.

"May I help you?" asked Secretary Octoblob. Secretary Octoblob was one of the few alien staff members. He/she/it? had eight suction-pad arms, which were always brimming with phones, rosters, charts, staplers, and an occasional student who came too close and couldn't get unstuck.

"We're here to see Principal Quark," Lani said.

"Did you do something bad?" he/she/it? asked.

"No."

"Did you do something *really* bad?" he/she/it? asked.

"No."

"Did you do something really, really, *really*—"

Lani straightened. "We would like to see her about an important proposal. Concerning her policy about holidays."

Secretary Octoblob's eye widened. "Holidays? Proposal? *Now?*"

"Yes, please."

"Oh, this should prove quite interesting. I'll buzz

you right in." As he/she/it? reached for the button, a student caught in an arm broke free.

"Finally!" Flash gasped, shooting away.

"Oh, hey, Flash," I said. So *that's* where he'd been.

Principal Quark's office was down a cold, dark hallway. When we came to the end, a steel door slid to the side. Then another slid up. Then another from the other side. Then a spiky iron gate. Beyond it was dark and misty.

"Uh, maybe we should come back," I said. "Like, in a *thousand* years."

"Just go," Lani said, nudging me forward.

Once inside, our eyes began to adjust to the darkness. Something lurked behind the desk, making a terrible hissing and sputtering sound.

"Principal Quark?" Lani said to the desk. "Is that you?"

"Huh? Wha?" The lights suddenly came on, and Principal Quark's eyes popped open. She blinked a few times. "What's going on?"

Lani cleared her throat. "I think we, um, woke you."

The principal's face reddened. "I was not *asleep*. I was deep in thought. I am a very deep thinker."

I winked. "I like to *think* too."

She looked me over. "It doesn't particularly show. Anyway, now that you're here, and I'm in a foul mood, please tell me what you want."

Lani pushed me forward. "Yes, tell her what we want, Bob."

"Me? But I, uh . . ." I pushed Beep forward. "Yes, tell her what we want, Beep."

"Beep want more Beeps!"

"I mean," I whispered, "tell her the *yummy* you want."

Beep nodded. "Beep want blueberry!"

"Blueberry," Principal Quark said, "is available in the Servo-server."

Beep clapped. "Yay!"

"Oh, aren't you a cute one?" the principal said, smiling.

"She likes him," Lani whispered to me. "This is our opening. Do something."

I floated a few inches closer to the principal's desk. "I think what Beep *meant* to say—and please remember how very, very cute he is—is that what we all really want is Halloween."

Principal Quark slammed her hands on her desk. "Out of the question!"

"But why?" I asked.

"Simple, young Bob. If Astro Elementary began celebrating planetary holidays, there would be no end. Every day is a holiday somewhere. Do you really want a party *every single day of the school year*?"

"Definitely!" I said, turning to Lani. This was turning out great!

Lani hissed, "She was speaking *rhetorically*. You weren't supposed to answer."

"But it's Halloween," I said to the principal. "Can't you just make an eensy-weensy exception?"

"I am very firm on rules," she said. "There are no exceptions."

Maybe this wasn't turning out so great.

Lani pulled me aside. "S.C.A.R.E.S. is failing! What are we going to do?"

I shrugged. "Too bad there aren't *space* holidays."

Lani gasped. "That's it. Bob, you're a genius!"

"I am?"

"Well, not in math," she said. "Or in science. Or in any actual subject. But still." She spun to face Principal Quark. "You said we can't have any planetary-based holidays. But what about one that's based in *space*?"

The principal laced her fingers. "Continue."

"Well," Lani said, "there's this really interesting cosmic holiday called, uh . . ." She turned to me.

"Called, uh . . . ," I said.

"Called Astroween," Lani continued. "And, um, Astroween comes this time every year, on the very last . . ."

"Very *first* . . . ," I corrected.

"Yes, sorry, on the very *first* day of October."

"And what, please tell me," Principal Quark said, "does one *do* on Astroween?"

"All sorts of fun things," Lani said. "But mainly, on Astroween, kids dress up as their favorite aliens, to help celebrate the, um . . ."

"To help celebrate the diversity of aliens everywhere!" I said.

Principal Quark held us in her gaze for what felt like an hour. "Interesting," she said.

"Uh, but don't forget, Lani," I said, "to tell the principal about the most *important* part of Astroween."

"What could be more important than celebrating diversity?" Lani said.

"Earth to Lani," I whispered. "The *candy*."

Lani shot me a look. "Yes, I was getting to that part of Astroween where all the kids march from door to door and say . . . What do they say again, Bob?"

I gulped. I couldn't say *trick or treat*, because that was obviously from Halloween. And besides, wasn't it time to retire the trick part anyhow? Let's be honest here, no kid who goes through all the bother of dressing up wants some goofy dad who thinks he knows how to entertain kids coming up with some dorky . . .

"I'm waiting," Principal Quark said.

"Oh, right. Sorry. What they say is"—I glanced over at Beep, who was playing with a sock, and it gave me an idea—"sock or . . . sweet! Because aliens like socks." At least Beep did. "And kids like sweets!"

"See how inclusive it is," Lani said.

"And then people give the kids tons of free candy!" I added. "The end."

Principal Quark pinched her chin. "Hmm. Astroween. Intriguing. I'll have to think about it." She shut her eyes and immediately began to snore.

Lani sighed. "Well, Bob, we tried. But I guess it just isn't meant to—" She jumped as Principal Quark popped awake.

"I have considered your request," she said, "and since it violates no rules, we can give it a try." She picked up her phone. "I'll have my secretary make the arrangements. Anything else, children?"

"No. No, we're good."

"Then you may leave now. Quickly, I suggest, before the spiky iron gate cuts you in two. Have a nice day!"

SPLOG ENTRY #6:
Lanced a Lot

As we passed back through the front office, Secretary Octoblob was already juggling a dozen (well, eight) different Astroween-related preparation tasks.

"One day's notice," he/she/it? said to us. "Thank you, children, for *that*."

Out in the hall, we did somersaults in the air and slapped high fives (in the case of Beep, high *ones*).

"We did it!" Lani said. "We get to wear costumes! And we only had to change the name, date, and complete history of Halloween to do it!"

"Costumes, that's right!" I said. "How are we going to get cool alien costumes by tomorrow?"

"Beep know good alien dress-up," Beep said. He yanked on the frayed end of the sock he was playing with until it was a mess of yarn.

"What's that for?" I dared to ask.

He then bunched the yarn and stuck it on his head. "Me be Bob-mother! Very alien scary. Gaahhhhh!"

This time it was Lani who clapped. "Very good impression, Beep!"

"Okay, okay," I said. "And you can stop doing somersaults now."

Lani looked at me. "We're not doing somersaults."

"Oh. Maybe I'm just dizzy with happiness."

Lani took my hand. "You're trembling again. I think it must be from lack of proper nutrients. Luckily, we're right by the nurse's office."

"Not Nurse Lance!" I said.

Lani yanked me toward the door. "Bob, you're not going to scream now, are you? Like—how does that go again, Beep?"

Beep went, "Gaaahhhhhhh!"

Lani laughed. "Just perfect." Then she clamped her hand on my back and, to my horror, shoved me through the door. "See ya."

"Well, hello again, Bob," Nurse Lance said to Beep. "What seems to be the problem?"

"That's Beep!" I said.

Nurse Lance studied Beep closely. "Well, so it is. Remarkable resemblance."

"He's wearing an old sock on his head!" I said.

The nurse turned my way. "So, Bob, once again, please tell me, what brought you into this soothing chamber of healing?"

"Well, I guess it all began when—"

"Yes, that's quite enough," Nurse Lance said. "We'll just strap you in the cold, hard chair and stuff you full of medicine."

"No, wait, I . . . hey, that really *is* cold."

He put his stethoscope on my forehead. "Hmm, heartbeat very faint."

"That's my head!"

"Say *ahhh*."

"Ahhh."

He looked into my mouth and made a face. "Well,

there's the main problem. You have a gross dangly thing in the back of your throat."

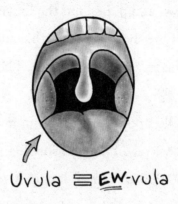

Uvula ≡ EW-vula

"That's always been there."

"Still, I should probably cut it out."

"What? No! My problem is sugar! The sweetenizer broke, and I don't have any hidden candy, and I'm just faint from it all! Please don't cut anything! Please!"

Nurse Lance nodded. "Ah, a simple sucrose imbalance. Why didn't you just say so?"

"Well, I tried to, but—"

"Fortunately for you, I have just the solution." He reached down and pulled out the longest needle I've ever seen! "One sharp jab from this and—"

"No, please, GAHHHHH! There must be another way!"

The needle stopped, inches from my neck. "Well, you *could* take a pill. Though I should inform you that it will take 0.00002 seconds longer to take effect."

"That's fine! Really! Anything but the shot. Anything!"

With a sigh, he put the needle away and unstrapped me. I felt a million times better already. "So," I said. "Where's my pill?"

He gestured to the medicine cabinet. "Take your pick. They all have sugar in them."

"They do?" I floated closer to inspect the selection.

"Of course they do. They're for children."

"But"—and I can't believe I was about to say this—"isn't sugar *bad* for you?"

He shrugged. "Eh."

I reached for a bottle that said TOOTHACHE MEDICINE. I had been having a little of that anyway. "What's the right dose? Will too much harm me?"

"Not at all. You see, once all the sweeteners are crammed into those pills, they have zero real medicine left."

"You mean, all this time . . . all this sugar . . . right *here*?"

He nodded. "Hope it helps, Bob."

I floated toward the door. "I'm sure it will, Nurse Lance. I'm sure it will."

SPLOG ENTRY #7:
Cosmic Costuming

After enjoying a dose or three of my new "medicine," I floated back into Professor Zoome's classroom, where everyone was already talking about the new space holiday.

I went up to Lani. "Who did you tell?"

"Only Zenith," she said.

Who obviously then told Andromeda. Who told

Flash. Who told Blaster. Who told Comet. Who told Hadron. Who told . . .

"Bob-mother!" Beep said. "Tomorrow Astroween!" Beep put the "Bob" wig on. "Sock or sweet!"

"Attention, class!" Professor Zoome yelled.

Everyone landed in their seats.

"No, not you, Bob," she said. "I need you up front."

Gulp.

"Bob," she said, "I know there's a lot of excitement about this rather suddenly announced holiday you told Principal Quark about called Astroween."

Double gulp.

"In fact, I've been researching it everywhere, and I can't find a single reference at all."

Triple gulp.

"And so, Bob, I need you to be completely honest with me about something."

What comes after triple gulp? Fourple? Purple? Vermilion?

"Yes, Professor Zoome?"

She pulled a bottle out of her desk. "What I need to know is: Should I put glittery blue streaks in my hair to dress up as one of the sixty queens of Venus? Or should I encase my head in a large brain to represent the telepaths of Einsteinium-7?"

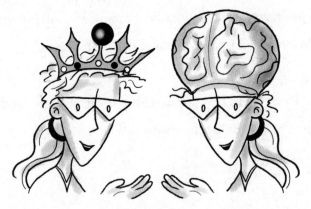

I shuddered at both thoughts. But at least I wasn't busted.

"I think in the time-honored spirit of Astroween...," I began.

"Yes?" she asked.

"You should do what you think is best."

Before she could respond, Beep swooped down and grabbed her bottle. "Blue glittery, yum!" And then it was gone.

"The big brain thing sounds cool," I said. "A definite Astroween winner."

"Then that is what I shall be." She turned to the class. "Well, what are you waiting for? We have but one day to prepare. Class dismissed!"

As Beep, Lani, and I floated down the halls, classroom doors swished open all around us. Word had spread fast. The entire school was in full Astroween prep mode.

"This is great," I said. "We should make up a new holiday every day. Especially now that my 'medicine' is gone." I tossed the empty bottle.

Lani caught the floating bottle and stuffed it in her pocket. "No excuse to litter." She then turned a corner. "Quick. We need costumes. And I know just the place."

"Me too," I said. "Astrozon Prime will ship overnight to anywhere in the solar system. And it only costs a sideways 8!"

"That's infinity, Bob."

"Oh." I was glad I wouldn't be home when Mom got the bill for those socks I had overnighted after Beep ate my last pair. "So where *are* we going to order our costumes?"

"Silly Bob. We're not going to *buy* our costumes." She slowed in front of the art room, and I had a very bad feeling about what she was going to say next. "We're going to make them!"

Okay, it's embarrassing to admit, but art is probably my worst subject (not including math, science, reading, music, and PE). The waxy feel of crayons gives me the jitters. And I still have nightmares about that time I got a glob of papier-mâché down my shirt.

"Create time, yay!" Beep said. He, of course, is amazing at drawing. Plus, he loves to eat blue paint.

"C'mon. It'll be fun," Lani said, pulling me inside.

The art room was already packed with desperate kids who also must have maxed out their parents' bank accounts. Ms. Splatz, the art teacher, turned to greet us.

She smiled. "Hi, Beep. Hello, Lani." Her smile faded. "Bob."

Okay, so last week I may have spilled a large can of brown paint. Sue me already.

"We're here to make costumes," Lani said.

"You and half the school! It's wonderful. I've set up paint in that area, beads and feathers in that one, tentacles and pipe cleaner antennae right there, and for those of you who *aren't* afraid of papier-mâché, a station in the back."

I cringed at the sight of big blobs of papier-mâché floating next to strips of torn newspaper. (Newspapers were how people got their news back in prehistoric times on Earth.)

"Let's go to the painting station," Lani said. Sadly, the paint was bobbing around in little globules too, mixing with the feathers and beads. The school should

probably splurge on gravity for the art room, too.

Lani grabbed a brush. "I'm going to make a costume in the style of the indigenous large blue people of Pandemonium. What about you, Bob?" Lani asked.

"What kind of alien species are you going to be?"

"Let me think. Which kind have the coolest laser blasters?"

"You can't have laser blasters with your costume! But you can choose something else." She grabbed some fluffy feathers.

"No way," I said.

"How about these tentacle things?"

I picked one up. It was squishy, sticky, and gross. "Double no way." But as I was putting it down, I noticed that some beads and other stuff were already stuck to it.

And then, possibly for the first time ever, I had a pretty good idea.

SPLOG ENTRY #8:
Bob-Monster

Okay, so maybe lugging eight tentacle-thingies back to my room wasn't the easiest task, but I knew it was going to be well worth it. After Lani and Beep helped me, I told them my plan.

"It's very nice, Bob," Lani said, "that you're going to be celebrating the species of Secretary Octoblob. I'm sure he/she/it? will appreciate it."

"Yeah, and think how many candy bags I'll be able to carry with all these! Eight arms times about ten suction cups on each arm times fifty pieces of candy in each bag equals"—I calculated with all my might—"two thousand yummy treats!"

"Four thousand," Lani said.

"Yes, but I always eat half before I get home."

Beep clapped. "Bob-mother candy math good!"

I shrugged. "Numbers have *some* uses."

I peeled a tentacle that was stuck to my back. "These things sure are hard to use. Maybe I don't need so many."

Lani sighed. "But then you wouldn't be honoring Secretary Octoblob. And it's such a nice gesture, considering how lonely he/she/it? must feel."

"Why would Secretary Octoblob feel lonely?" I said.

Lani leaned in and whispered, "You'd be lonely

too, if you were the only one of your species around."

I pointed at Beep. "Beep is the only one of his species around, and he's okay." I slapped him on the back. "Aren't you, buddy?"

But Beep was suddenly not looking so okay. "Beep try hard forget." His big eyes welled up. "But now Bob-mother remind."

Lani glared at me. "Now look what you did."

"Beep sad!"

Lani leaned to hug him. "There, there, Beep. Just because Bob is an insensitive monster, doesn't mean you have to cry."

"Hey, what did I do?"

Lani grabbed a box of tissues. "Here, Beep. Use these."

Beep gulped the blue box down. "Lani-friend nice."

"I'm nice too," I said. "Remember, I'm the one

who lets you call me 'mother,' even though I'm clearly not."

Beep's eyes got teary again. "Bob-mother not Beep mother?"

Lani kicked me. "Of *course* he's your mother. Isn't that right, *Bob*?"

I gritted my teeth. "Yes, Beep. I'm your new mother. Are we all happy now?"

Beep clapped. "Beep say yay!"

Lani put her hand on Beep. "Nothing's more important than family and friends, Beep."

"Especially on Astroween," I added.

"Beep wish more Beeps come for sock or sweet," Beep said. "Bob-mother bring?"

I wasn't about to break it to him that even if I knew where to find his home planet, I doubted one of his siblings would make an intergalactic trip for a made-up holiday. But I felt I owed him, so I said, "I'll tell you what, Beep. I'll send out an invitation. Just promise me you won't get your hopes up."

Beep bounced. "Hopes up! Hopes up!"

I went to my computer and opened Spacebook, which is how we post random messages out to space. "What should we say?"

Beep thought for a moment. "Hmm . . ."

"Make it honest," Lani said. "Sweet, but not too sappy. Simple, but not too—"

"CANDY FREE COME! CANDY FREE COME!" Beep said.

I typed that in and hit enter.

"And now that that's done, let's get ready," I said. "Because no matter what happens, one thing's for sure: Tomorrow is going to be the best Astroween ever!"

SPLOG ENTRY #9:
Beep Bag

I woke in my dorm room extremely relaxed and refreshed. I stretched my arms and knocked on the bunk above. "Beep, you awake?"

He peeked down. "Beep wake. Bob-mother wake?"

"You can *see* I'm awake, Beep. In fact, it was the best night's sleep I've had in ages. Probably because I slept so bad the night before." I floated out from the covers. "At least it's still early. It would have been a nightmare to oversleep on Astroween."

"No early," Beep said. "Past lunch."

"It's not past lunch, Beep. Look." I pointed at the starry night out the window. And then I remembered it was always like that!

Beep held up the bedside clock. "See. Day."

"*One thirty!* Oh no! Beep, why did you let me sleep so long?!"

"Bob-mother like sleep."

"Yes, but not *today*!"

"Plus, Bob-mother cute when sleep."

"Quick, we have to get in costume!" When Beep put his "Bob" wig on, I added, "I mean, me. Help *me* get all these awful tentacles on."

It wasn't easy. Every time I got one attached, it would stick to others. Before I knew it, all the tentacles were balled in a slithery, sticky mess.

"This is useless!" I kicked at the tentacles, and they suctioned off my shoe. Finally, I settled for wearing one. "There. Do I look like an alien?"

"Bob-mother always look alien."

That was good enough for me. I faced the door. "Then what are we waiting for?"

"For Bob-mother brush teeth?"

"Sheesh, Beep, who has time for that? Let's go!"

To my horror the Astroween activities were already in full swing at school. I pushed through the crowded hall.

"Bob, Beep, there you are!" Lani called. "I've been

looking for you everywhere." I turned toward her voice and saw a sleek purple girl with big ears and a tail.

"Wow, is that you?" I said. "Your costume looks so real."

She smiled. "Thanks. Took me about three hours to apply the paint alone." She glanced at the one limp tentacle sticking out of my chest. "What happened to the other seven?"

"Long story."

"But you were supposed to dress as an *actual* alien species."

"Hey, I tried!" I said. "So, what have I missed?"

"The costume parade, zero-grav apple bobbing, an Earth bounce, pin the antenna on the space donkey, bag decorating . . ."

"The candy! Have I missed any candy?!"

She held up her bag (decorated with glitter, felt stars, glitter, googly eyes, math equations, and more glitter). "Just started. Grab a bag and join me!"

"Will do!" I looked around. "Where are the bags, anyway? I'll need about ten."

She led me toward the bag decorating station. "Uh-oh. Looks like they're all gone. See what happens when you sleep in?!"

"There must be something I can use." A backpack

or pillowcase would do, but those were both back in my room. I glanced around. At Beep. At the empty table. At Lani. And then back at Beep.

"Beep, little buddy! How much can your pouch tummy hold?"

He spread his arms. "Beep hold lot and lot more!"

"Perfect!" I said. "Beep, will you be our Astroween candy bag?"

"Beep bag! Beep bag!"

"Great," I said. "Let's fill you up!"

SPLOG ENTRY #10:
Ding, Dong

I have to say, the next hour was one of the best of my life. There we were, three friends on an October school day, going from classroom to classroom and saying, "Sock or sweet!" Teachers opened their doors and poured all sorts of yummy candies into our bags (or, in my case, into Beep). It was glorious.

"C'mon, Beep, what are you waiting for?" I said as

he stopped to look out a window. "We have two more floors to go."

He kept his eyes on the stars. "When more Beeps come?"

"I told him not to get his hopes up," I whispered to Lani.

"I feel terrible," she said.

"Then eat some candy."

She looked in her bag, then wrinkled her nose with disgust. "I don't even *like* candy."

I shuddered. "Do I even know you?!"

"Well, mint gum, maybe," she said. "I haven't had any of that since leaving Earth. But all this—"

Beep interrupted with a happy cry, and "Beeps come! Beeps come!"

I turned. "What?"

He pointed out the window at an approaching fleet of small ships. "Beeps come for Astroween! Beep go let in." Then he took off.

"Wait for us, Beep! You don't know who they are!"

But Beep was fast. By the time we caught up to him at the air lock, the first ship was already docking. It clanked into place and whooshed steam. (Space sounds are cool.)

The air lock bell then chimed *ding, dong, ding.* (Okay, not all space sounds.)

I peered out the portal. "I can't see anyone. They're too short."

"Like Beeps! Like Beeps!"

"Maybe," I said, "but school rules say that we're really not supposed to let anyone in until . . ."

Beep hit the button and the door slid open. (He's never been one for school rules.)

And before I could say hello, I found myself in the clutches of a long, slithering tentacle.

SPLOG ENTRY #11:
Sugar Blues

The good news is, I didn't die. You can tell I didn't die because I'm still writing my splog. FYI, a sudden STOP in my splog = bad news.

But even though I didn't die, it wasn't exactly pleasant being gripped by a long, slimy tentacle. Especially because the tentacle pulled my face close to the extremely slimy and ugly (let's call it slugly) face of an alien.

"M-may I help you?" I said.

"Take. Us. To. Your. Sugar!" it demanded.

"S-sugar?"

Lani, off to the side, said, "I think it means leader. Take us to your *leader*."

"I mean *sugar!*" the alien said, squeezing me harder.

"Here!" Lani said, holding out her bag. "Take all the candy you want."

"Oooh," the alien said, and tossed me aside. He looked in the bag, then handed it to another one like him. For the first time, I noticed they all had only one tentacle each, coming out of their chests.

"Hey, I'm dressed as one of you." I turned to Lani. "See!"

"To mimic our kind is an insult worthy of death!" the alien said.

I yanked the tentacle off and chucked it. "Not mimicking! Not mimicking!"

I'm still writing my splog, so you can see my plan worked.

The alien with the candy bag said, "This is not nearly enough. We need more."

Lani leaned in to whisper, "Whatever we do, Bob, we better not tell them about Astroween."

"I'm not going to tell them about Astroween." I turned. "Are you, Beep?"

"Beep no tell Astroween." He turned to one of the aliens. "You tell Astroween?"

"Not me," the alien said. Then: "Wait, what is Astroween?"

The chief alien, who I'll just call Sluglyface, said, "Do not try to deceive us. We received your invitation. CANDY FREE COME, it said."

"Good going, Bob," Lani muttered.

"Hey, you were there too!"

Sluglyface turned to his forces. "Search the entire station. Take every morsel you find!"

"Wait. *Every* morsel?" I said.

"Looks like you're not the only one with a sweet tooth, Bob," Lani said.

Sluglyface gasped. "You *eat* the candy?"

"Uh, you don't?"

"Sugar is the fuel we use to run our fleet," he said. "To eat such a poison is un*thinkable*."

Suddenly more and more aliens poured through

the door. Soon the school was going to be swarming with them. Unless I thought of something. And fast.

"It's too bad there's not an emergency intercom on the wall," I said to Lani. "Then we could warn everyone."

"But there *is* an emergency intercom on the wall." She pointed. "Right behind that big alien guard."

I shrugged. "Well, so much for that idea."

"Bob, don't be so gutless! All I have to do is distract him."

"Wait, Lani . . . !"

But she had already floated up to the guard. "Oops, silly me," she said. "I seem to have lost a gumdrop."

"Hmm, must find it," the guard said, and bent to look.

"NOW, BOB! GO!"

Before I could talk myself out of it, I shot toward

★ 295 ★

the intercom and hit the red button. It crackled to life.

"Attention, everyone!" I said. "Astro Elementary has been invaded by candy-stealing aliens! Anyone who looks like a candy-hungry alien is an invader! Hide all your candy and fight for your lives!" A tentacle then covered my mouth, and I found myself being tossed back toward Lani.

I brushed my hands together. "Well, that was pretty amazing of me, I must say."

"Bob," she said. "You dolt! Today *everyone* looks like a candy-hungry alien!"

SPLOG ENTRY #12:
We're Goo

O kay, so my poor choice of words may have started a mass panic. What can you do?

As if things couldn't get worse, some more of the aliens then pushed some kind of contraption through the door. It had a big opening at the top and a spout at the bottom.

"What's that?" I asked.

Sluglyface put his hand on it and grinned. "This is the Gooifier."

"And what does a"—gulp—"Gooifier do?"

Sluglyface leaned so close, I could smell his slugly breath. "It *gooifies*." He then took Lani's bag of candy and tossed it inside.

"NO!" I said, but I was too late. The Gooifier made chopping, gurgling, and popping sounds (Gooifier sounds are cool too.) And then: plop. Goo came out of the spout.

Sluglyface held up a full jar. "Behold: perfectly pure rocket fuel."

Or perfectly pure candy syrup. "I don't suppose I could, uh, taste it?" I asked.

Sluglyface grimaced, then turned to his soldiers. "Now take the Gooifier to the dining hall. And bring the prisoners!"

Minutes later we were roughly herded into the cafeteria. And not just us: lots of dazed-looking kids, teachers, and even Principal Quark (who looked like she had been woken from some very deep "thinking" time).

But even worse, right in the middle of the room was every candy bag in the school. They were going to gooify it all!

I couldn't help but shudder as bag after bag was tossed inside and chopped, gurgled, popped, and plopped into goo. At least I still had *my* candy safely hidden inside Beep. When every crumb was gone, Sluglyface counted the jars. "This is not enough. We need one more to power our fleet!"

Principal Quark stepped forward. "You've taken it all. Now go."

"There must be a bag we overlooked!" Sluglyface said.

Next to me, Beep began to say, "Beep bag! Beep b—"

I clamped his mouth. "Beep, shhh!"

But it was too late: Sluglyface had heard. He approached Beep. "You dare to conceal candy from us?"

Beep patted his tummy. "Beep bag for Bob-mother."

Sluglyface's eyes gleamed. "You heard him. Throw the little alien in!"

"Who alien?" Beep said.

"You are *all* aliens," Sluglyface said.

"Beep no alien! You alien!"

"Since when are *we* aliens?" Sluglyface said.

"Since born."

"Pah, this is pointless. Throw him in now!"

I jumped forward. "No! You can't!"

"And *you* can't stop us!"

That was probably true. Not by fighting, anyway. But how, then? As they took Beep away, they held us all back.

"Bob, we have to do something!" Lani said.

"Like?"

She slipped away and ran.

But can I blame her? After all, it wasn't Lani's fault we had gotten into this mess. (Actually, it was

Mr. Da Vinci's; if only he had fixed the sweetenizer when it first broke, then we never would have had to make up a new holiday that somehow led to this hostile invasion.)

And yet, in a small way, it was my fault too. So before I could talk myself out of it, I pulled free and said, "Wait, no! Take *me* instead."

Sluglyface chuckled. "But you are not a candy bag."

"Listen, mister," I said. "I've been eating nothing but sugared cereal, syrup, jelly, soda, and caramels since I was old enough to open a refrigerator. And that's just for breakfast! The truth is, I'm probably more sugar than boy. Not that I'm proud of it, and if I somehow survive this, I vow to eat *healthy* from now on, but for now I—"

"Enough already," Sluglyface said. "Throw them *both* in."

"GAHHHHH!" I screamed as a tentacle swooped me up and held me directly over the machine.

Which I know sounds bad, but as long as you're still reading this, it means I . . .

SPLOG ENTRY #13:
Sweet Surprise

Oops, sorry about that. Just dropped my splog-o-matic recording tablet. Right at the exciting part too.

Anyway, as I was saying, as long as you're still reading this, it means I didn't get turned into goo! (Beep didn't, either, in case you were wondering.) I mean, sure, it seemed touch and go for a minute there, but just as my head was dangling over the little choppers, I heard the cafeteria door swish open, and a voice yelled, "HERE! HERE'S ALL YOU NEED AND MORE!"

I pulled myself up just in time to see . . . Lani! Carrying an overflowing bag! While I assumed she had run away for good, she had really broken free and found some more sweets. But where?

To answer, Nurse Lance darted up behind her, screaming, "NOOOOOOOO! That's the school's entire supply!"

"It's one hundred percent sweetener," Lani said. "Does the medicine even work?"

"No," he admitted. "But at least children take it."

He *did* have a point.

Sluglyface swiped the bag away. "This will do nicely. Let those two go."

Beep and I broke free of the tentacles and shot away.

"Yay Lani!" Beep said.

After they had all the fuel they needed, the aliens began to pack up.

"And now we will leave," Sluglyface said, "and not return until this very day next year and on every day you call Astroween from now on in order to replenish our supplies."

Oh, great, just what we needed. A yearly shake-down. But just as I was about to give up hope of ever eating candy again, Mr. Da Vinci stepped forward to study the Gooifier.

"Interesting," he said. "Looks like you don't need sugar at all for your fuel."

"We don't?" Sluglyface said.

Mr. Da Vinci bent down. "See this switch here? You have

it set to SUGAR. But with one little flick . . . there. Now it's set to SALT."

"But how will that help us?"

"Well, for starters, the dried ocean beds of Hydrocon-Six have more salt for the taking than you could use in a million years."

"My sister-in-law lives on Hydrocon-Six!" Sluglyface said. "This is most welcome news."

Mr. Da Vinci shrugged. "I do what I can."

"You are a genius," Sluglyface said. "Perhaps you would consider joining us on our journeys."

"What, and leave all these children I have come to know so well?" Mr. Da Vinci said. He then threw down his mop. "Finally, someone who appreciates me! Ciao, kids, ciao!"

And so they finished packing and left, never to bother us again (???????).

« ∗ « ✪ » ∗ »

Afterward, I stood with Beep and Lani in the empty cafeteria.

"So how did you know about the medicine?" I asked Lani.

"Before I recycled the bottle you tossed, I read the ingredients on the side."

"At least it all ended happily," I said.

"It did?"

"Sure. The aliens got their fuel. Mr. Da Vinci got a new job away from milk-spilling kids. And I"—I patted Beep—"still have some candy."

"But, Bob," Lani said. "You vowed to eat *healthy* from now on if you survived."

"Hey, you were at the nurse's office when I said that."

"Actually, I was waiting right outside the door when you made your little speech."

"Waiting for what? They were about to kill me!"

"I know," she said, smiling. "Which means my dramatic timing was perfect!"

I folded my arms. "Okay. Well, at least everyone *else* is happy."

Lani nodded toward Beep. "Not everyone, Bob."

"Beep?" I said to him.

Beep sniffed. "More Beeps no come after all."

"Oh, Beep, it'll be okay." I looked at Lani. "Won't it?"

She gave me a look that said I better make this right.

"Um, I just remembered," I said, "there's something I have to do. Lani, how about you bring Beep to Professor Zoome's classroom in about twenty minutes?"

I then flew out of the cafeteria and down to the art room. I quickly cut a bunch of construction paper and made it back to Professor Zoome's just ahead of Lani and Beep. I hovered in front of the door as they tried to come in.

"Before you come in, Beep," I said, "shut your eyes."

"Then Beep no see."

"It's a surprise."

"Oooh, Beep like surprise!"

Lani led him to the center of the room, and the entire class surrounded him.

"You can open your eyes now."

Beep's eyes widened as he saw that each one of us was wearing a pair of Beep arms (or flippers or flappers or whatever they're called).

"You don't need more Beeps, Beep. We're your family now," I said. "And to you we all say . . . yay!"

Everyone lifted their Beep arms. "YAY!"

Beep smiled, then grabbed me in a big hug.

"Who needs sweet," Lani said, "when we have Beep!"

I started to raise my hand, then lowered it when she shot me a look.

Because she was right. I may not have had any candy. But I had my good friends.

And so ended what really was the best Astroween ever.

SEND

Bob's Extra-Credit Fun Space Facts! (Even though nothing is fun about space!)

On **Earth**, every day is a **holiday** for someone somewhere! (Though they tell you about only some of them, so you don't get too many days off school.) Holidays usually come once a **year**, but here's the wild part: Since a year = the amount of time it takes for a **planet** to travel once around its **sun**, if you go to other planets, years are totally different lengths!

Like on **Mercury**, for example, one year = about 88 Earth days! Compare that to 365 and a quarter days for one Earth year, and think how rushed things must feel on Mercury. The baseball season probably has only about forty games (which is still *way* too many), and summer vacation must be over in a blink (though summer vacation *every*where is over in a blink).

On the other hand, since a **day** = the amount of time it takes for a planet to rotate one time on its **axis**, one day on Mercury = about 58 Earth days! Which means that if you ever moved to Mercury, you could probably pop a giant bowl of popcorn and spend an entire Saturday watching *all* the *Star Wars* movies in order, from *Episode IV* (IV is *Star Wars* for

"4 but really 1") to *Episode ZZZZZ* (which is *Star Wars* for "I fell asleep after they blew up the 600th Death Star").

Wait—does Mercury even *have* Saturdays?

Double Trouble

SPLOG ENTRY #1:
Hard Work Is Hard!

Dear Kids of the Past,

Hi. My name's Bob and I live and go to school in space. That's right, space. Pretty sporky, huh? I'm the new kid this year at Astro Elementary, the only school in orbit around one of the outer planets. There's just one micro little problem:

GETTING GOOD GRADES HERE IS NEARLY IMPOSSIBLE!

I mean, back on Earth at my old school, I got a trophy for learning how to Velcro my shoe. But if you dare ask the teachers here for a little help putting on your space helmet the right way so your head doesn't explode, they deduct six points from your grade average and make you sharpen pencils for a week!

Beep just clapped and said, "Head go pop, yay!" Beep is a young alien who got separated from his 600 siblings when they were playing hide-and-seek in some asteroid field. Then he floated around space for a while, until he ended up here. Sad, huh?

You know what's even sadder? I was the one who found him knocking on our space station's air lock door and let him in. Now he thinks I'm his new mother!

On the bright side Beep not only likes sharpening pencils but also most of the other mind-numbing tasks I give him. Which frees up my time to do more important things like . . . like . . . like . . .

"Bob-mother like sleep late!" Beep said.

Well, who doesn't?

Beep is also really good at drawing, so I let him do all the pictures for these space logs (splogs, as we call them) before sending them back in time for you to read. Beep says to tell you that he once was terrible at drawing, but that he worked really hard and that you can too. (Unlike me, of course, who was smart enough to give up art the second I realized I could draw only stick figures!)

Anyway, I promise to try to write more entries soon, maybe between my after-school nap and my predinner rest time.

Enjoy!

SPLOG ENTRY #2:
Sad and Sadder

Okay, so things didn't go exactly as planned. Somehow, I accidentally napped through dinner, and then I accidentally played video games for four hours, and now it's past midnight and I still haven't started my giant homework project that was assigned only two weeks ago and is suddenly due tomorrow.

Beep patted his tummy as he floated across the

dorm room we share. (Sadly there's no gravity in space.)

"Din-din yummy tonight," he said. "Beep eat for Beep, and Beep eat for Bob-mother, too."

"Why didn't you wake me?"

"Bob-mother look cute when drool on pillow."

No one had ever called me "cute" before. But that was beside the point. "Listen, Beep, we have to focus on this project. Are you going to help me or what?"

Beep clapped. "Or what!"

"Help me look for the work sheet with the assignment written on it." I opened a drawer, and a bunch of papers and junk floated out.

"This work sheet?" Beep said, holding up a floppy manila time-velope.

"No, that's for mailing our splog journals to the kids of the past."

Beep studied the time-velope. "Mail Beep and Bob-mother to past too?"

"We'd have to be two inches tall, Beep, to fit in there. Besides, those aren't meant for mailing people."

Beep shoved the time-velope in his pouch. "This work sheet?" he said, holding up a crumpled paper.

"That's the one!" I grabbed it from him and read. "All we have to do is build an accurate model of a famous structure, such as the Eiffel Space Tower, using ice pop sticks."

Beep clapped again. "Ice pop sticks, yay!" Ice pops were kind of Beep's weakness.

"The best model in the class will be chosen to represent our school at the Ice Pop Stick Finals on Earth's moon. Which, you know, actually sounds kind of fun. I've never been to the moon."

"Beep neither."

I lowered the paper. "I've also never won anything. I wonder what that's like, to win a contest in front of everyone. With all the kids and teachers gazing up at you and everything. It must be the best feeling ever."

Beep clapped. "Bob-mother win prize! Go to moon!"

"Well, not *yet*. But I suppose there's a chance. If we work really hard."

"Bob-mother no like work hard."

"That is a problem." I straightened with resolve. "But you know what, Beep? We're going to do this project thing, and we're going to do it well. Okay, first we need about ten thousand ice pop sticks."

Beep raised his hand. "Oo, oo! Job for Beep! Job for Beep!" He spun. "Where ten thousand ice pop for Beep eat?"

"Sorry, Beep, that's not how it's done. Professor Zoome gave me *one* ice pop stick"—I reached into my backpack—"and this duplicator ray."

"Ray not look yummy."

"That's because it's a tool, not a treat. Watch." I

let the ice pop stick float, aimed the duplicator, and pushed the button. A yellow ray zapped out. Suddenly, there were two floating sticks.

"See, Beep. Now we just have to do it"—I tried to subtract two from ten thousand in my head—"about ninety thousand and eight something more times." (I'm not so great at math.)

Beep folded his arms. "Beep like eat ice pop better."

"Well, we don't have ten thousand ice pops. So this will have to do." I handed the ray to Beep. "Here, you work on that while I start gluing the sticks together."

Beep immediately pointed the ray at my head. "Idea more better! Make two Bobs. Then work go two time fast!"

"No, Beep, wait—"

He pushed the button. *Click.*

Beep pouted. "No work."

"That's what I was trying to tell you. Duplicator rays are designed to work on objects only. Not life-forms."

"Bob life-form?"

"Yes, I'm a life-form!"

Beep pointed the ray at my desk. "Desk life-form?"

"No, but—"

Zap! Suddenly, there were two desks.

He pointed at the dresser. "That life-form?"

"Beep, we don't need another—"

Zap!

"Pillow life-form?" Beep said.

Zap! Zap! Zap!

"Stop that, Beep! This room is crowded enough!"

"Beep life-form?" He pointed at his foot.

Click.

His face grew sad when it didn't work. "But Beep want more Beeps."

"Sorry, Beep, that's not how it works."

He unscrewed a panel on the back of the duplicator ray, exposing the wiring inside. "Beep have idea! Beep switch blue and red wire!"

I shot forward. "Beep, stop fiddling with that! You don't know how it works."

Beep put the panel back on. "Now Beep make ray work on life-form!"

"Give me that!" I said. But as I yanked it away, my finger may have brushed the button . . . just as the ray was pointed at Beep!

Zap!

"Oh no!" I froze. "What have I done?"

Beep looked down at himself and pouted. "Ray still not work on life-form. Beep sad."

Next to him, another Beep nodded. "Beep Two *sadder*."

"Here tissue," the first Beep said, turning.

The second Beep dabbed his eyes.

And I promptly passed out.

SPLOG ENTRY #3:
Trouble Times Two

My eyes opened to the sight of Beep patting a wet cloth on my forehead.

"Thanks, Beep," I said. "For a second there I thought you had—"

A second Beep patted me with another wet cloth.

"Gaaahhhhh!" I said. "Beep, what have you done?!"

They looked at each other. Then the truth finally

hit them, and the two Beeps squealed, high-fived, and hugged.

"Guys, keep it down!" I said just as there was a knock on my dorm room door. It was followed by a voice: "Bob, are you okay in there?"

I pointed to the bunk bed. "Quick," I whispered to the Beeps. "Hide!"

Beep took his normal spot on top while, annoyingly, the duplicate Beep took *my* bed.

I opened the door a crack. "Oh, Lani, hey," I said.

Laniakea Supercluster is my best human friend at Astro Elementary. She's smart, cool, and fun, so I do my best to also act smart, cool, and fun whenever she's around. (The key word there is "act.")

"What's going on?" she said. "I was passing by and heard all this commotion."

"Oh, that was just Beep making some noise," I said. "And me. And Beep. I mean, Beep making more noise. *Not* a second Beep."

She gave me a funny look.

"So," I said, trying to change the subject, "what are you doing up so late?"

"Homework," she said.

"Me too!" I admitted. "After all, our ice pop stick thingies are due in just a few hours."

"Not *that* assignment, Bob. I finished that ages ago. I'm studying for my final exams for eighth grade."

"Eighth grade! But that's"—I counted on my fingers—"sixteen years from now!"

She laughed. "Not quite."

Beep and Beep giggled from the bed. I tried to talk loudly so she wouldn't hear them. "Speaking of science," I said, "I was wondering: What would happen if someone, uh, switched the red and blue wires on a duplicator ray, and accidentally zapped their little buddy?"

Lani thought. "Theoretically, switching the wires could allow for animate organic matter, or *life-forms*, to be duplicated too. But as I said, only theoretically."

The Beeps giggled again.

"So if someone *theoretically* duplicated someone," I went on, "it would be pretty easy to reverse, right?"

She pinched her chin. "As far as I know, the

creation of matter cannot be reversed without risking total annihilation of the universe. Why do you ask?"

I gulped. "No reason. Well, nice talking to you. Good night!"

I felt bad about closing the door on her, but I was in a near panic. I shot around the room. "Quick, Beep, I'll throw away the duplicator ray, and you get rid of the extra Beep."

The other Beep floated out from the sheets. "Get rid of Beep Two make Beep Two sad." He flashed those big Beep eyes.

"Listen," I said, "I'm really sorry, but . . . would you stop looking at me like that?!"

"Bob-mother mean," Beep said.

Beep Two nodded. "We need new Bob-mother," he said, and promptly grabbed the duplicator from my hands.

I lunged forward. "NO, WAIT, I—"

Zap! A yellow flash blinded me. Then all I saw were blinking spots. But as those faded, a face came into focus. A face that looked exactly like mine.

"Hello, Bob," the other Bob said.

"Oh, hey," I answered back. And once again passed out.

SPLOG ENTRY #4:
Backward Bob

When I opened my eyes again, I tried not to freak out at the sight of the other me who was staring right back.

"This. Is. Weird," I said.

"Rather," the other Bob replied.

I studied him for a moment. "Do I really look like that?" I asked.

Beep Two shook his head. "No, new Bob-mother more handsome."

Original Beep nodded. "More handsome much!"

"But we're the same!" I said.

"Not *same* same," Beep said. "He backward."

I studied him closely. "He doesn't look backward to me. It's like staring into a mirror."

My reflection folded his arms. "Exactly. And reflections are *flipped*." He grabbed the duplicator from Beep Two. "It appears someone switched the red and blue wires, reversing the polarity, which not only reverses the life duplication settings, but it also *reverses* what it duplicates."

"And make backward Beep and Bob-mother!" Beep said.

"Backward or not," I said, "mistakes were made, and we have to focus on a way to *un*make them."

"Throw old Bob-mother out space station door?" Beep Two offered.

Original Beep nodded. "May be only way."

"Whoa, wait!" I said. "Let's not be hasty. In fact, maybe there's a positive side to all this."

Backward Bob lifted an eyebrow. "Such as?"

"Like"—I thought for a second—"Beep and I can sleep in and play video games while the new Beep and Bob go to class."

Beep clapped. "Idea good!"

"And every night when we have to do homework," I went on, "our duplicates can do it for us!"

Beep clapped again. "Idea *super* good!"

"And when we get assigned to go on a hazardous space mission . . ."

"All right, we get the point," Backward Bob said. "It's a deal."

I blinked in surprise. "It is?"

"Why ever not?" he said. "After all, you gave us life. Helping you out is the least we can do. I am you, right?" His eyes glinted, and he arched an eyebrow.

"If you really insist," I said, "you and Beep Two

can make our ice pop stick model while we sleep. It doesn't have to be perfect, just best in the class and then better than anyone's at the finals. Got it? Thanks!" I stretched and yawned. "Nice meeting you, backward me. See you in the morning!"

I put my head on my pillow, and in a second I was out.

I woke with a start, not knowing if it was day or night (a problem with living in space), so I rubbed my bleary eyes until the clock came into focus. When I saw the time, I sprang up.

"Beep, why didn't you wake me?!"

"Bob-mother look cute when drool on pillow *again*."

Could I help it if I was so cute? I shot out of bed. "Quick! We're going to be late for class!"

"But Backward Bob-mother already go."

I froze. "So that wasn't a dream? There really is another me?"

"And Beep!"

"Hmm," I said, "this could be a pretty sporky turn of events. You know what this means?"

"Seem good now but then get worse and then end very, very bad?"

"It means, Beep, that for the first time all school year, we're going to have a nice, leisurely breakfast."

Beep clapped. "Strawberry waffle time, yay!"

And, without rushing for once, we were off.

SPLOG ENTRY #5:
Space Jam

About a half hour later Beep and I patted our bellies.

"Breakfast is actually good, Beep, when you don't shove it down in ten seconds."

"Beep shove for thirty minute!" He belched strawberry jam.

I stretched my arms. "So what should we do now, Beep? Morning nap? Or video games? Or . . . or . . ." I tried to think of a third option but came up blank.

"Beep miss class. Beep want go say hi."

"I don't know if that's such a good idea. Don't want to interrupt our doubles, you know."

"What if just look?"

I thought about it. "No harm in spying, I suppose," I said. "Okay, let's do it."

We floated from the cafeteria to our classroom. As we arrived outside the door, I heard Professor Zoome saying, "Very good, Bob! Very good indeed!" followed by lots of clapping.

I peeked inside. Everyone was gathered around a giant ice pop stick model of the Eiffel Space Tower.

"It's beautiful, Bob," Lani was saying. "But how did you get all those colorful little blinking lights inside?"

"It wasn't all me," Backward Bob said. "I used this Temporary Shrink Ray to reduce Beep to a one-inch height, and he ran strands of decorative lighting from bottom to top. He also installed a working elevator and a replica of the actual Eiffel Space Tower gift shop, complete with tiny overpriced T-shirts."

"Very good, Beep!" Professor Zoome said.

"But late last night you'd barely even started," Lani said to Backward Bob. "How did you complete it so fast?"

"That's true," Backward Bob said, "which is why Beep and I decided to stay up all night and even skipped breakfast. Great work demands great effort."

Lani looked a bit suspicious, but everyone else clapped. *Oh, please.*

"Not only do you earn a stellar grade, Bob," Professor Zoome said, "but due to the results of the Clap-O-Meter, it is clear that your model will represent our school at the Ice Pop Stick Finals this evening on Earth's moon. And I believe you have a very good chance of winning the coveted Platinum Ribbon and trophy! We will make a class trip of it later this afternoon."

I turned to Beep. "Did you hear that?" I whispered. "He's getting all the credit!"

"Backward Bob-mother did do all work."

"Yeah, but . . . but . . ." It still didn't seem fair. I cleared my throat and entered the room. "A-ahem."

Everyone spun and gasped.

"Oh no," Lani's friend Zenith said. "Not *two* of them."

Professor Zoome folded her arms. "Can someone please tell me what's going on?"

"Uh, just a little duplication incident," I explained. "What can you do?"

"Yes, what can you do, Bob"—Professor Zoome turned—"and Bob?"

"Actually, from now on," I said, "you should probably just refer to me as 'Bob' or 'Bob Prime,' and call that one 'Backward Bob.' This all goes into my splog, and I really don't want to confuse my readers."

"I'm sure they are plenty confused already," Professor Zoome said.

I patted Backward Bob on the back. "Anyway, thanks for finishing my tower in time for the big competition. I can take over from here." I eyed the Eiffel Space Tower model and smiled.

"Hey, you can't take credit for that," Zenith said. "The *other* Beep and Bob are the ones who made it."

"Yeah," I explained, "but Beep and I made *them*."

"And *I* made the classroom rules," Professor Zoome said, pointing to a poster on the wall.

I gulped. "Did I mention it was kind of an accident?"

She pointed again.

I slumped. "So now what?"

"Now, Bob," she said, "you will be marked tardy and you will take your seat.

Only you have no seat, since it is currently occupied by your double, so you will have to jam into one space together."

Beep clapped. "Jam, yay! Beep like strawberry."

Beep Two clapped. "Beep Two, too!"

I hung my head and mumbled, "Could this morning get any worse?"

"And once you are seated," Professor Zoome said, "please clear your desk for a pop math quiz."

And there was my answer.

SPLOG ENTRY #6:
Bad Breaking

In case you're wondering, it's pretty awkward having to share a desk with yourself. Especially if you're a chair hog.

I raised my hand. "Professor Zoome? Backward Bob is pushing me off my seat!"

"My pardons," Backward Bob said. "But I was only doing so because he keeps trying to copy my answers." He shot me an evil glare.

Professor Zoome gasped. "Bob, I am very disap-
pointed you would cheat off another student."

"But he's not another student. He's me!"

"No, Bob," she said, "he is your *reverse*. You are impulsive; he exercises self-control. You rush through work; he takes his time. Your hair gets poofier on your right side; his gets poofier on his left."

"Poofier?" I said.

"Moving along," Professor Zoome said, "in light of today's *incident*, we will review objects in nature that come in doubles. Can anyone give me an example?"

Lani raised her hand. "A double star. Which is when two stars are near each other, forming one system." She smiled. "You get two sunsets. Now *that's* pretty."

Zenith raised her hand. "Double helix. Which is the name of a twisting molecular shape that forms things like DNA."

"Excellent," Professor Zoome said. "Any more?"

Beep raised his hand. "Ooh, ooh! Double ice

cream scoop! Beep love double ice cream scoop!"

Professor Zoome sighed. "Obviously, this lesson is at an end. Please line up for music class, and don't forget to bring your transdimensional flutes."

Well, surprise, surprise, Backward Bob turned out to be a better flute player than I am, a better science student, *and* a better cometball player. He was even better at lunch—he picked healthier foods and chewed his food longer!

By the time we had to leave for the moon (to cheer him on for his *awesome, amazing project*), I was pretty much not in the mood.

"Class," Professor Zoome said, "please proceed to the Astrobus docking bay. Blastoff is in ten minutes."

I eyed Backward Bob, who was struggling to get his Eiffel Space Tower model through the Astrobus door. "Spin it left," he said to Beep Two. "No, other left!"

Spotting my opportunity, I quickly floated over. "Need some help?"

"You can help by floating into a black hole," he said.

Not to be discouraged, I grabbed one of the tower supports near the bottom. "The simplest way to fit it through the door would be to"—I twisted with all my might—"*break it!*"

The class gasped.

"Bob," Professor Zoome said, "what are you doing?"

"Nothing," I said. "I'm just trying to"—I gave the model a chop—"destroy this thing!"

Lani pulled me away.

Blaster the bully pointed. "Ha! He didn't even damage it."

I didn't?

Backward Bob folded his arms, and his eyes did that glinting thing again. "Poor, weak Bob."

"Hey, if I'm weak, you are too."

He leaned close and grinned. "I'm you *backward*, remember?"

"I've seen enough!" Professor Zoome said. "Lani, please escort Bob to the office. He won't be joining us on our trip."

"Why do I have to take him?" Lani said.

Professor Zoome smiled. "Because you are trustworthy and responsible."

Lani blushed. "Oh, right. C'mon, Bob, let's go."

"But . . . but . . ."

Lani leaned close. "Don't make it worse. It'll be

okay. At least Beep is sticking by you." She glanced around. "Beep?"

I spied him next to Beep Two. "Beep, get over here!"

I hung my head and let her take me away.

SPLOG ENTRY #7:
Deep, Deep, *Deep*

don't get it, Bob," Lani said after we floated for a minute in silence. "Why were you trying to sabotage Backward Bob's chances of winning a Platinum Ribbon and becoming one of the most famous students in the history of Astro Elementary?"

"Yeah, he is a real moon-rock-head, huh?"

Lani stopped. "You're jealous."

"Why shouldn't I be? He's good at everything! And I'm good at . . . at . . ."

"Yes?"

I slumped. "See, that's just it. I'm not good at anything!"

"Oh, Bob, that can't be true. You're good at, uh, uh, uh . . ."

"See."

"Lunch," she said. "You're good at lunch!"

"But he's better!"

"Bob, life isn't all about the fact that your duplicate—and, okay, everyone else at this school—is better than you at everything. You're forgetting what's most important."

"Breakfast? Because I'm good at that, too."

She looked me in the eyes. "Bob, of everyone I

know, you're the best at simply . . . being good."

"Huh?"

"Think about it," she said. "You were the one to open the air lock door for Beep and rescue him when he was lost. And now you look after him like a big brother."

"Bob-*mother*," Beep corrected.

"And when my pet spider Zilly was floating toward the black hole, it was you who saved her." (You might have to see some of my earlier splog journals to know what she's talking about.) "And when I needed cheering up the other day, you told me all those silly jokes."

"That was my life story."

"Whatever. The point, Bob, is that deep down—"

"Deep, deep, *deep*!" Beep added.

"—you're a really good guy."

A warm feeling rose from my stomach (probably

shouldn't have put so much hot sauce on my waffles). But no, it wasn't indigestion. It was something else.

"Being good at doing things is nice, Bob," Lani said. "But being good *to others* is better."

I blushed. "Gee, Lani, thanks."

Beep clapped. "Bob-mother good! Bob-mother good!"

Lani smiled at me. I smiled at Lani.

And then Lani's smile faded.

"Oh no," she said.

"What?"

Her eyes grew wider. "OH NO!"

"What?!"

"If deep down *you're* very good, then deep down Backward Bob must be—" She spun. "We have to stop the Astrobus! NOW!"

And we were off.

SPLOG ENTRY #8:
Dancing Pirates?

We shot as fast as we could back to the Astrobus docking bay, and made it just as Backward Bob was carrying his Eiffel Space Tower through the bus door.

"Someone stop him!" Lani called.

But no one heard us because they had already boarded. Backward Bob shot us an evil glare as he turned, blocking the entrance.

"So, I suppose you've figured it out," he said.

"I've figured enough," Lani said. "If deep down Bob is good, then at your backward little core—"

"I'm rotten as a bad apple!" Backward Bob finished. "Yes, you've discovered my true nature. But you may not have guessed my brilliant plan."

"Probably not," Lani said. "Why don't you waste time like all villains by slowly explaining it to us?"

He smirked. "Nice try. But the bus is ready to go, and off to the moon I must be. And what a nice view the moon has of the Earth, that pathetic little planet. All I have to do now is to aim this duplicator ray Earthward"—he held it up—"and I will create a beautiful but horrible backward Earth of my own!"

Lani gasped. "An evil Earth?! But what's to stop it from it taking over Earth Prime?"

Backward Bob raised his arms and cackled.

"With me as its leader? Nothing!! Bwhaaa-ha-haaaaaaaaaaaa!"

Next to him, Beep Two added, "Bwhaaa-ha-yay!"

The bus door slid closed, locking us out. Backward Bob waved through the window. "See ya. Never again!"

The Astrobus engines began to roar.

"Uh-oh, we better get out of here," I said. I yanked Lani and Beep out of the docking bay and closed the door just as the Astrobus blasted out with a fiery whoosh.

Instead of thanking me, Lani put her hands on her hips. "When he was giving that long talk, you were supposed to grab him!"

"How was I supposed to know?"

"I was flashing you the signal behind my back!"

"I thought you had an itch."

Lani sighed. "Either way, now they're gone, and we have to think of a plan of our own."

I thought for a minute. "I've got it! All we need is another duplicator ray, plus a freeze ray, a heat ray, a cupcake ray—in case we get hungry—about two dozen dancing pirates, a sixty-foot-tall android—make that *three* sixty-foot-tall androids—a starship, a ninja mask, a . . ."

Beep clapped. "Plan good!"

"You haven't even heard it all yet. But it's foolproof!" I said. "As long as we can get those two dozen dancing pirates." I slapped my forehead. "But where in the galaxy are we going to get dancing pirates at this hour?"

Beep pouted. "Plan bad."

"Wait, I have another idea!"

Lani had already reopened the docking bay door. "I have a *better* plan," she said, leading us to one of the parked buses. She opened the bus door.

"Quick, get inside," she said.

I stared at her in shock. "Whoa, Lani, I never thought of you as the type who would steal an Astrobus." She had a bad side. How cool!

"What are you talking about?!" she said. "I would never steal a bus! I'm using the interbus communicator to warn Professor Zoome."

"Wait," I said, "does that mean you *don't* have a bad side?"

She rolled her eyes. "Are you going to help me or what?"

Beep sat in the driver's seat and started playing

with the steering wheel. "Beep go vroom, vroom!"

Lani reached for the communicator controls. "Calling the Astrobus headed for Earth's moon. I repeat, calling the Astrobus headed for Earth's moon. Come in."

The speaker returned nothing but static.

"You sure you have the right channel?" I asked.

"Yes! Look, it's the only bus listed in flight right now. They're halfway to Earth already!" She tried again, but still nothing.

"Backward Bob must have switched the channels off," I said. "He's just so evil."

"Beep go after Backward Bob!" Beep said, spinning the steering wheel again.

"Stop playing with that," I said. "You might accidentally turn it on."

"Silly Bob-mother. Wheel no turn bus on." He

reached for a green button. "Green button turn bus on!"

The engines sparked to life.

"Beep, turn that *off*!" Lani yelled.

"Okay, turn," Beep said, spinning the wheel. He hit the accelerator. "Then *off*!"

The Astrobus careened in circles around the docking bay, narrowly missing the walls.

"GAAAAHHHHHHHHHHHHHH!" I yelled. I pointed to the bay doors, which had slowly begun to open. "Straighten, Beep! Straighten!"

He sat taller in his seat. "Beep posture bad," he admitted.

"STRAIGHTEN THE *SHIP*!"

Beep yanked at the wheel, and we shot through the narrow gap of the doors . . . right into space.

SPLOG ENTRY #9:
Moon Mall Fifty-One

We all exhaled. "That was close," I said.

"Well," Lani said, "looks like we have a new plan. Can you fly this, Beep?"

Beep touched the navigation screen, revealing icons of the planets. "Which one Bob-mother want go to? That one? Or that one? Or *that* one?"

I gazed at the icon of the blue-green planet

I knew so well: my home. "Earth. Take us to the moon of Earth."

Beep did as I said. The ship's computer announced, "Estimated flight time fifteen minutes."

I slumped. "Fifteen minutes. That's like forever!" I studied the control panel. "Can we get any games on this thing?"

Beep shook his head. "No game."

"Movies?"

Beep cried, "No movie, either!"

I began to panic. "What are we possibly going to do for fifteen minutes?!"

"Ahem," Lani said. "We *could* use that time to work out our plan. I still don't understand how dancing pirates fit in."

I shrugged. "I forget. Anyway, when it comes to plans, Beep and I pretty much like to wing it."

Beep flapped.

About fourteen long, boring minutes later, the bus began to slow.

"We're approaching Earth," I said.

The beautiful blue marble grew closer. I pointed at the white moon in its orbit.

"Take us there, Beep."

When he tapped the control panel, a list of the most important moon landing destinations popped up.

"Moon Mall One," Beep read. "Moon Mall Two. Moon Mall Three. Moon Mall Fo—"

"Is there anything other than malls on the moon?" Lani asked.

I scanned down the list. "Moon Mall Forty-Nine. Moon Mall Fifty. Wait, here it is: Moon Educational Auditorium (soon to be Moon Mall Fifty-One). That's it, Beep! Take us there as fast as you can, with only one brief stop at Food Court Eleven!"

"Food court, yay!"

I pictured Backward Bob making an evil duplicate Earth and gritted my teeth.

"On second thought, Beep, we can do the food court *after* we save the planet."

Beep gasped. "Bob-mother sure?"

"Well, maybe if there's a drive-through . . . No, Beep, my decision stands. To the educational auditorium!"

SPLOG ENTRY #10:
And the Winner Is . . .

Sadly, it took a while to park. Astrobuses were descending into a giant glass dome from every direction.

"Beep beep!" Beep said to the buses in our way.

"There's a spot." Lani pointed, and Beep swerved the bus into the space and popped open the door.

"Watch your step," Lani said. "There's gravity on the moon, though it's only one sixth of Earth's gravity. So each step is like one big bounce."

I grabbed Beep by the foot. "Did you have to tell him that?"

All around us, kids were bouncing from their buses to the giant building, carrying all sorts of ice pop stick models.

"Look," Lani said, "there's a model of Big Space Ben, and one of the Great Space Sphinx. And it looks like that entire class re-created the stone monoliths of Spacehenge!"

All great space monuments were basically great Earth monuments with the word "space" in them. Probably to keep things simple.

Over all the heads, I spotted a bobbing Eiffel Space Tower. "Look, that must be our class!" We zigzagged through the crowd and caught up just as they were about to enter the auditorium.

Professor Zoome did not look happy to see us. "Bob, I thought I sent you to the office!"

"You did, but . . . but—"

Lani took over. "We came to warn you: Backward Bob has a horrible plan to make an evil, duplicate Earth! You have to stop him!"

Professor Zoome raised an eyebrow toward Backward Bob, who was struggling to get his tower through the auditorium door. *"Him?"*

"He does seem kind of bumbling," Lani admitted, "but that's just an act. He's actually razor sharp, highly motivated, and ruthless—the opposite of *real* Bob."

"I'm good deep down," I pointed out.

"Deep, deep, *deep*!" Beep added.

"And I think, Bob," Professor Zoome said, "that not so deep down you're envious of his success. I'm sorry, but unless he appears to pose an actual threat, the show must go on." She spun to bounce away. "See you inside."

We followed the crowds into the auditorium. Everyone was setting up their models on rows and rows of long tables.

"What now?" I said.

Lani shrugged. "You heard Professor Zoome. Not much we can do until Backward Bob makes a move. In the meantime, we might as well enjoy ourselves. It's not every day we get to come to such an important educational competition."

"Oh, yay," I mumbled.

Lani stopped to admire a model of the Empire Space Building. "Ooh, I bet this one has a good chance of winning a ribbon."

I caught sight of the Eiffel Space Tower an aisle over. "There he is. Let's sneak up and surprise him!"

"No, wait!" Lani cried.

But I had taken matters into my own hands. I ducked down and approached from behind, and just as he didn't expect it . . .

"BOO!" I yelled, jumping out. "Got you!"

A boy who looked about five years old started to cry. An older girl next to him put her hands on her hips and scowled. "How dare you startle my little brother like that! He worked for weeks on his model, and now you come along to ruin it!"

"I . . . I'm sorry," I said. "I thought he was an evil version of me."

The girl rolled her eyes. "Sure, that's what they all say."

Lani pulled me away. "I was *trying* to tell you: There are dozens of Eiffel Space Towers here."

I reddened. "Let's check somewhere else."

Fortunately, our luck turned. Out of nowhere I caught a whiff of popcorn! I raised my head. "Look, Beep—snack bar! Let's go!"

And we were off!

A few minutes later, we were catching popcorn kernels in our mouths and keeping an eye out for Backward Bob.

"Shh," Lani said. "They're about to announce the winners."

The auditorium lights dimmed, and a voice boomed over the loudspeakers: "Welcome to the Ice Pop

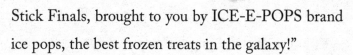

Stick Finals, brought to you by ICE-E-POPS brand ice pops, the best frozen treats in the galaxy!"

"Oooh," Beep said.

"While all of the entrants are winners in a small sense," the announcer said, "only three are *actually* winners, as chosen by the judges of Planet Pops

Incorporated, makers of the best frozen treats in the galaxy!"

"Ahhh," Beep said.

The announcer continued: "The third place Uranium Ribbon goes to: Stella of Starbright Academy, for her model of the Empire Space Building!"

A spotlight shone on the model and its maker, who was being hugged by all her classmates.

"Told you that one was good," Lani said.

"In second place, a Plutonium Ribbon will be awarded to: Newton of the Lunar Lab School for his model of the Levitating Space Tower of Pisa!"

"Mmm, pizza," Beep said.

"Backward Bob's entry is as good as those," Lani said. "If he wins this thing, then we just have to follow the spotlight and we'll have him."

A loud drumroll sounded, and lights flashed in

all directions. "And now the moment you've all been waiting for: To get your free coupon for ICE-E-POPS brand ice pops, just enter promo code G-O-T P-O-P on our intergalactic website now!"

Everyone cheered and took out their phones.

"Oh," the announcer continued, "and the Platinum Ribbon and special first place trophy goes to Bob of Astro Elementary."

Squeals erupted a couple aisles over.

I pointed. "Let's get him!"

SPLOG ENTRY #11:
Ribbon Blues

Lani, Beep, and I rushed to the spot where the prizewinning Eiffel Space Tower gleamed in the spotlight. Professor Zoome and all my classmates were whooping and clapping. Lucky Backward Bob. Why couldn't that be me?

I stopped. "Where is he?"

Everyone's clapping slowed. They glanced around,

puzzled. A judge held up a sparkly ribbon. "Where is the winner?" she said.

"No worries, I'm sure he'll be here momentarily," Professor Zoome answered before hissing to the class, "Has anyone seen him?"

"Uh-oh," Lani said. "I have a bad feeling."

"Beep, can you spot him?" I said.

Beep bounced. "No there." He turned and bounced again. "No there." And again. "No there." Another bounce: "There! There!"

"Backward Bob?" Lani gasped.

"Backward Bob-mother *and* Beep Two at snack bar!" Beep added. "And now they leaving with popcorn bag. Rush to exit!"

"Good job, Beep!" Lani said. She grabbed my arm. "Let's go!"

But I didn't move. Lani stopped, puzzled. "What's wrong, Bob? Aren't you coming?"

But I could focus only on the judge, who was tapping her foot in annoyance. "If this Bob of yours doesn't show up soon," she said to Professor Zoome, "we'll be forced to award the prize to someone else."

I took a step in her direction.

"Bob!" Lani called. "If we don't go now, he's going to get away!"

I eyed the Platinum Ribbon. It was so glittery and beautiful. I'd never won anything, let alone the grand prize. And they *had* called for Bob of Astro Elementary.

The judge spotted me. "Ah, you must be Bob. Finally."

Professor Zoome shrugged. "Close enough." The class seemed confused, but they applauded anyway.

The judge leaned toward me and smiled. "In the name of Planet Pops Incorporated, makers of the best frozen treats in the galaxy, I hereby present this award to the most deserving, hardworking student of the year. Congratulations!"

The ribbon seemed to come at me in slow motion, like in those movie scenes where the hero has to make

a very important decision and the audience is left in suspense.

"Sorry, my arthritis is acting up again," the judge said. "In just one more second I'll have this on you. Make sure to smile. This is likely going to be the most special moment of your life."

I could feel the entire auditorium about to erupt in cheers. How amazing was it going to feel?

I swallowed. "Beep helped too, so I really can't take *all* the credit."

I eyed Beep, hoping he was enjoying this as much as I was. But the second he saw me, he looked away. "Beep no say yay."

And that's when I knew what I had to do.

Just as it touched me, I brushed the ribbon away. "Sorry," I said. "But as much as I want this, I don't deserve it. You'll have to give it to someone else while I go stop the evil me!"

The judge rolled her eyes. "I so much preferred judging dog shows."

"C'mon, Lani and Beep!" I said. "Nothing can stop us now."

SPLOG ENTRY #12:
Outside the Dome

Well, maybe something could stop us. Like getting to the exit and realizing Backward Bob was long gone.

"This is all my fault," I said, kicking at the ground.

Lani nodded. "Sure is."

Beep nodded. "Sure is."

"Don't know what you were thinking," Lani said.

"Don't know what Bob-mother thinking," Beep said.

"If he ever thinks at all," Lani said.

"If Bob-mother ever—"

"Okay!" I said. "I get it." I kicked at the ground again.

Beep bent over. "Careful, Bob-mother! Almost kick yummy popcorn!" He picked a kernel up and tossed it in his mouth.

"You shouldn't eat off the ground, Beep," I said.

Beep nodded and bent again. "Bob-mother have next one." He tossed another kernel my way.

I watched as it slowly floated down. "Wait, Beep. Are you thinking what I'm thinking?"

Beep clapped. "Strawberry jam world?"

"No, the popcorn." I pointed ahead. "Look, it

makes a trail! Backward Bob must have spilled some as he got away!"

"Kernels smart!" Beep said.

Lani smiled at me. "Bob is smart too. Sorry if we sometimes forget."

"It's okay," I said. "Let's go!"

Lucky for us, eating popcorn while bouncing on the moon made for lots of spills. The trail led around the back of the building.

"Careful," Lani said, "he could be hiding near those Dumpsters."

"The popcorn leads that way, toward the edge of the dome," I said. "But why?"

Lani squinted. "There's an air lock door. He must have gone outside!"

We rushed toward the dome and pressed our faces

against the glass. Sure enough, two figures were leaping up a high hill on the lunar surface, leaving a trail of dusty clouds.

"I don't get it," I said. "Where are they going?"

"Oh no," Lani said. "Once they get to the top of that ridge, they'll have a clear sight of it."

"Of what?" I said, but I had already guessed the answer.

Lani went pale. "Of Earth."

SPLOG ENTRY #13:
Lani, Too

I didn't love the thought of going outside the safety of the glass dome into the airless atmosphere of the moon, but we had no choice. Luckily, there were some extra helmets and gloves in the air lock. We suited up quickly and opened the door.

"Once Earth is in view," Lani said, "he'll be able to aim at it with the duplicator ray!"

"If only we'd never started goofing off with that

ray to begin with," I said. "Though that probably would have made my splog entries a lot more boring for my readers."

Beep nodded. "This no boring. This fun!" He leaped extra high. "WHHEEEEEEEEEE!"

Lani and I followed. Each leap brought our feet down into the soft dust, scattering it slowly in big puffs. "This *is* kind of fun," I agreed.

"We better pick up the pace," Lani said. "They're almost there."

Ahead of us, a bright disc began to rise over the crest. A beautiful blue-green world.

"Earth," I mouthed. I hadn't been home since leaving for Astro Elementary at the start of the school year.

Two silhouettes stepped in front of my glowing home world. One of them had the outline of a duplicator ray in his hand.

DOUBLE TROUBLE

"No, you can't!" I shouted, scrambling over moon boulders as fast as I could.

Backward Bob looked down at me. "Sorry, Bob, old friend," he said, his voice coming through my helmet radio. He turned and lifted the duplicator ray toward Earth. How could we stop him?

"Think about what you're doing!" Lani called up. "If you push that button, then . . . actually, I forget what's supposed to happen. Maybe if you could explain it all to us again. And be sure to start at the beginning."

"Hey, smart thinking, Lani," I said. "And this time I'll remember to grab him."

"Nice try," Backward Bob called out. "But I'm going to push the button now."

"NOOOO!" I yelled.

"NOOOO!" Lani yelled too.

"WHHEEEEEEEEEE!" Beep yelled, bouncing forward like a rubber missile and hitting Backward Bob's arm with full force.

A yellow ray zapped from the duplicator, but thankfully not at Earth.

"You did it, Beep!" I said.

"Yes, silly little alien," Lani said. "You *did* do it. I thank you much!"

It seemed like a funny thing for Lani to say. I turned to see what was going on.

"Uh, Lani," I said, "why am I seeing two of you?"

"Because," Lani said, eyes wide, "the ray accidentally hit *me*! And now there's an evil me, too!"

"Oop," Beep said.

"Well, hello there," Backward Bob said to Evil Lani. "Interested in ruling a backward world together?"

Evil Lani smiled as she approached him. "Hmm, tempting." Her smile faded. "But not really," she added as she chopped his arm, causing the duplicator ray to spin her way.

"Don't worry," she said as she caught it. "I promise not to do something as pointless as shooting a mere planet."

"Whew," I said.

Evil Lani pivoted, aiming the ray into the sunlight. "Not when I can crown myself the terrible queen of my own double *star*!"

And before anyone could stop her, she pushed the button.

SPLOG ENTRY #14:
Shrinking Hopes

Everyone gasped as a yellow ray zapped toward the bright ball of fire in the dark lunar sky.

I squinted, looking near but not directly at the sun. To my relief, there remained only one big star. "Whew, nothing happened," I said.

Evil Lani huffed. "But my aim was true! What a piece of junk," she added, tossing the ray against a boulder, where it split with a crack.

Original Lani raised her arms. "Doesn't anyone get it?! Just as it takes light 8.3 minutes to travel from the sun to the Earth, it will take 8.3 minutes for the duplicator zap, moving at 186,282 miles per second over approximately 93,000,000 miles, to reach the sun!"

"Huh?" I said. Math *really* wasn't my thing.

"It means that very soon we're going to have two suns," Lani said, "and with the gravimetric pull of a double star system, the orbits of all planets will change, and Earth will go spinning into oblivion!"

"Um, one more time," I said.

"WE'RE ALL GOING TO DIE!" Lani yelled.

That I got.

"But I still get to be star queen, right?" Evil Lani said.

Backward Bob shook his head. "Sadly, she's not very bright."

Lani nodded. "She's a backward me, remember."

"This really has gotten way too complicated," I said.

"It's not that complicated, Bob," the real Lani said. "The speed of light is a widely known universal constant. In fact, because stars are so far away, when you look in the night sky you're actually looking back in *time*."

"Cool," I said. "But too bad I can't *go* back in time. Then I'd stop myself from duplicating Beep and starting this whole mess to begin with."

Lani gasped. "Bob, wait. You're a genius!"

"I am?"

"Well, maybe not *genius*," Lani said. "But it's a great plan! All you have to do is shrink yourself and mail yourself back in time just in time to warn yourself not to duplicate yourself!"

"I can do that?"

"Well, theoretically," Lani said. "Though, like all things that have never been tried, it would be extremely dangerous."

I gulped.

Lani sighed. "But it hardly matters, because we would need a time-velope *and* a Temporary Shrink Ray, and where are we going to find those in the few minutes we have left?"

Beep reached in his pouch. "Beep have time-velope!" he said, pulling out the one he'd put in earlier.

"Great! But what about a Temporary Shrink Ray?" Lani said.

Backward Bob, standing by a big moon rock, began to cackle. "Oh, you mean like *this* one?" He then pulled it out of his space belt and pointed it at the rock. *Zap!* The rock shrunk to pebble size. "I've been carrying it around ever since I shrunk Beep Two to work on our ice pop stick project."

"I don't suppose we can borrow it?" I said.

He cackled again. "Not even if you say 'please.' Because now I have a *new* evil plan!"

"Oh yeah?" Lani said. "What is it? And please don't omit any details as you slowly explain your plan."

"Well, first of all," Backward Bob said, "I'm going to shrink Evil Lani, because I'm very unhappy that she chopped my arm. Then I'm going to shrink you, Bob, and have Beep put you in his pouch. Then I'm going to shrink Beep and"—as he went on and on, Lani gestured wildly at me.

"Wait, what does that mean again?" I asked. "You have an itch?"

Lani sighed. "Fine, I'll do this," she said, and with one giant moon leap she swooped down and yanked the Temporary Shrink Ray right out of Backward Bob's hands.

She then bounced over to grab the time-velope from Beep. "Quick, I'll shrink you and Beep and send you back to your room last night."

"But . . . but . . . ," I stammered, not exactly liking the thought of being shrunk *or* sent through time. Before I knew what was happening, a green light flashed, and everything seemed to grow around me.

"GAAAAAAAHHHHHHHHHH!" I cried as Lani's gigantic hand scooped me and Beep up and slid us into the time-velope. She then sealed us into darkness.

Beep clapped. "Tiny Beep and Bob-mother go on ride, yay!"

To: BOB'S ROOM

1:00 A.M.

GO

DOUBLE TROUBLE

I pushed against the narrow walls. "Not yay, Beep. I'm scared of tight spaces! And why does it smell like old socks in here?"

"Beep use extra time to arrange sock collection."

"This ride better be smooth!" But just as I said it, everything began to spin and spin and spin, and I screamed.

Our journey to the past had begun.

SPLOG ENTRY #15:
So Confusing

"WHHHHEEEEEEEEEEEEEEE!"
Beep said as we spun back in time in the
dark and cramped time-velope.

"Beep, if we survive this, I'm going to make an important vow."

"Never give up?"

"Never get out of bed!"

I moaned as we twirled and twirled, strange lights blinking and flashing all around.

"Beep think big adventure make Bob-mother grow."

I nodded. "Now that you mention it, having to deal with my bad side has helped me with some personal growth."

"No, Beep mean Bob-mother GROW."

My limbs pressed against the tight inside walls of the time-velope. "It is getting less roomy in here. The shrink ray must be wearing off!"

Beep looked down. "Beep start grow too!"

My head pressed against the inside top of the time-velope, causing my neck to bend. "We have to stop this thing, Beep!"

"But no off button!" Beep, also expanding, pressed into me.

"Stop being such a time-velope hog!" I said. "It's getting too tight! I can't breathe! It's also going faster! And faster! And FASTER!"

"WHHHEEEEEEEEEEEEEEEEEEEE!"

"The sides are starting to split! This is it, Beep, this is—!"

The time-velope burst open, dumping Beep and

me into the middle of . . . our dorm room!

Over by my desk, I saw *me* holding a crumpled piece of paper and saying, "All we have to do is build an accurate model of a famous structure, such as the Eiffel Space Tower, using . . . HEY, WHO ARE YOU?!"

"I'm *you*," I said. "From the future!"

"Cool," Past Me said. "Quick, tell me who wins the next Galactic Series. If I bet the right way, I can be rich!"

"No idea," I said. I yanked the paper from his hand and fed it to the paper shredder. "All I know is that you and Beep can't start your ice pop stick project. And you especially can't use the duplicator ray!"

"You mean this one?" Past Me said, pulling it out.

I grabbed the ray and tossed it in the paper shredder too. Which caused the shredder only to spark and jam, but still.

I turned to Beep. "Beep, we did it! We came to the past and prevented ourselves from duplicating ourselves! Now there's no Beep Two and no Backward Bob and no Evil Lani and everything can get back to normal!"

"Actually," Past Me said, "with you two here, there *are* now two of each of us."

I slapped my forehead. "I can't stand this anymore! Okay, I'll tell you what." I pointed at Past Me. "You're going to temporarily shrink Beep and me and put us in a time-velope. Then you're going to send us back to the future."

"But aren't our duplicates in the future?" Past Me said.

"Well, just send us ahead five minutes or something," I said. "As long as you don't use the duplicator ray, our duplicates won't exist."

"But isn't there another Bob five minutes from now?" Past Me asked.

"No, because *we're* the future us!"

"Wow," Past Me said. "Time travel is so confusing."

"Best not to think too hard about it," I agreed.

"Beep make chart," Beep said, handing me a diagram of our plan.

"Guess it checks out," I said.

And even though it didn't involve dancing pirates, that's what we did.

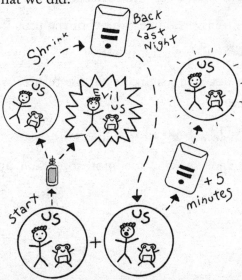

SPLOG ENTRY #16:
Making the Grade

Okay, Beep and I are back in our room now, five minutes ahead of the past Beep and Bob we'd just left.

I let out a big sigh. "Now, Beep, it's *really* over. Whew!"

"Double whew!" Beep said.

I smiled. "Maybe too soon for *double* anything, Beep."

Beep clapped.

I suddenly felt my weariness. "All right then," I said with a stretch. "I think we'll sleep well after all the excitement."

Beep picked up the original ice pop stick. "But what about project?"

"I don't think . . . ," I began, but then I remembered how it felt to almost win a ribbon. Maybe, just maybe, I *could* try a little harder.

"Okay, Beep. But this time we're not using any fancy rays. We're doing it the old-fashioned way," I said. "Eating lots of ice pops!"

Beep clapped. "Plan good! Plan *double* good!"

Even with Beep's help, I knew we'd never have enough for a truly award-winning project. But then I remembered something else. I rushed to the door and opened it just as Lani was passing by.

"Oh, hey," I said. "You're up pretty late studying for your eighth-grade finals."

Her eyes widened. "How did you know?"

I shrugged. "Lucky guess."

Beep giggled.

"Anyway," I continued, "I was wondering if you wanted to come in for a little snack? All the ice pops you can eat."

Lani smiled. "Sure, I could use a little break. Sometimes I wonder if I work *too* hard."

Beep giggled again.

And so we stayed up and ate ice pops, and by the time we were done, I had constructed a nice Eiffel Space Tower. It didn't have flashing lights, and it was so small, it fit in my backpack. But I was proud of it anyway.

"You know, deep down," I said, "I think I have

what it takes to get pretty good grades after all."

"Deep, deep, *deep*!" Beep said with a smile, and swallowed the last ice pop whole.

SEND

Bob's Extra-Credit Fun Space Facts! (Even though nothing is fun about space!)

Light is fast. Really fast. Really, really fast. Really, really, *really* fast. Really, re . . . okay, I'm writing "really" too much, but this report is supposed to be 200 words long. And that's a lot of words. I mean, it's really a lot of words. I mean it's really, *really* . . .

Anyway, if you want to get technical, light travels

at 186,282 miles per *second*. So in the time it takes for Beep to say "Yay-one-thousand!" light can go more than halfway from the Earth to the moon, even with a brief stop at the **Intergalactic House of Pancakes**. But even at that super speed, light from the closest star to our sun, **Proxima Centauri**, takes more than four years to get here, and light from the farthest known star, **Icarus**, takes over nine billion!!!!!

Sometime back in all that time long ago is when **dinosaurs** existed, but there are no dinosaurs in space. At least, there better not be. I used to think there were no spiders in space, but sadly I was wrong. I mean, I was really wrong. Really, *really* wrong. Really, *really*, REALLY . . . okay, I'm just about to 200 words. And now Beep is craving strawberry pancakes, so I better go. See ya!

Nancy Drew

✷ CLUE BOOK ✷

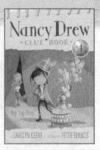

Test your detective skills with Nancy and her best friends, Bess and George!

NancyDrew.com

FOLLOW THE TRAIL AND SOLVE MYSTERIES WITH FRANK AND JOE!

HardyBoysSeries.com